"You simply don't understand!"

As she looked at Chad with a spark of anger in her eyes, Megan continued, "It's totally inconceivable to you that there are women in this world who need to love and know that they're loved in return before they'll go to bed with a man."

"Love!" Chad's lips curled back in a snarl. "Love is a disease of the mind, Megan, and if you're weak enough to succumb to it, then it makes you vulnerable."

"Love is a two-way commitment, Chad." Megan despairingly tried to reach him. "It involves fidelity and trust and—"

"Fidelity! Trust!" His expression was contemptuous. "To expect these two qualities from a woman would be as foolish as to come between a hungry lion and its prey...."

Yvonne Whittal, a born dreamer, started scribbling stories at an early age but admits she's glad she didn't have to make her living by writing then. "Otherwise," she says, "I would surely have starved!" After her marriage and the birth of three daughters, she began submitting short stories to publishers. Now she derives great satisfaction from writing full-length books. The characters become part of Yvonne's life in the process, so much so that she almost hates coming to the end of each manuscript and having to say farewell to dear and trusted friends.

Books by Yvonne Whittal

Don't miss any of our special offers. Write to us at the following address for information on our newest releases.

Harlequin Reader Service
901 Fuhrmann Blvd., P.O. Box 1397, Buffalo, NY 14240
Canadian address: P.O. Box 603,
Fort Erie, Ont. L2A 5X3

Bridge to Nowhere

Yvonne Whittal

Harlequin Books

TORONTO • NEW YORK • LONDON
AMSTERDAM • PARIS • SYDNEY • HAMBURG
STOCKHOLM • ATHENS • TOKYO • MILAN

Original hardcover edition published in 1989
by Mills & Boon Limited

ISBN 0-373-17064-5

Harlequin Romance first edition June 1990

Printed in U.S.A.

CHAPTER ONE

THE POST OFFICE technician and his assistant gathered together their intricate equipment and prepared to vacate Megan O'Brien's curio shop as the hands of the wall clock shifted towards five. Megan had remained calm throughout the day, taking their lengthy intrusion in her stride, but she was immensely relieved when she finally saw them leave.

It had taken several hours that day to install a telephone in the newly erected veterinary building, and it was now linked to the telephone in Megan's shop. She had not objected to this temporary arrangement, but Byron Rockford's dark eyebrows met above his tawny eyes in a display of glowering displeasure as he stood observing the departure of the two men.

'I'm sorry about this, Megan,' he muttered, directing his frowning glance at Megan's small, slender frame as he thrust his big hands into the pockets of his khaki pants and leaned his tall, wide-shouldered frame against one of the glass-topped display counters.

Megan waved aside his apology. 'It was my suggestion, don't forget,' she reminded him, the corners of her soft mouth lifting in a smile as she tilted her head back to meet his steady gaze.

Byron Rockford was a ruggedly handsome individual in his late thirties and the sole owner of the Izilwane Game Park. He was married to Megan's cousin Frances, and over the past three years Megan had succumbed to an affectionate warmth for this man who had become such a vital member of her adopted family.

'I've been wanting to have a word with you all day, but there've been so many distractions.' Byron smiled apologetically, his glance holding Megan's. 'I wanted to thank you for making my old bungalow habitable for our resident vet.'

Megan's wide, candid blue eyes could sparkle with laughter as easily as they could cloud with compassion, but at that moment it was curiosity that lay in their depths. 'Has he arrived?' she asked.

'Not yet,' Byron replied with a shake of his head. 'I had a call from Chad McAdam about an hour ago to tell me that he's been delayed and wouldn't be arriving at the camp until late this evening.'

Chad McAdam! This was the first time Megan had been told the name of the man who was to be the resident veterinary surgeon in the game park, and a tiny shiver of shock rippled through her. She had no reason to believe that this would be the same man she had met very briefly almost a year ago in Johannesburg when she had attended a function at the home of Revil Bradstone and his attractive wife, Alexa, but hearing the name Chad McAdam still seemed to have the power to shake her considerably.

'I'll have to arrange that some of the restaurant staff remain on duty until McAdam arrives,' Byron intruded on Megan's scattered thoughts, and she pulled herself together sharply.

'The restaurant staff deserve a break,' she argued calmly. 'My bungalow is right next door to the one Dr McAdam will be moving into, and it would be no trouble at all to prepare a meal and leave it in the oven in his kitchen.'

Byron hesitated, an odd look flashing across his face, then he shook his head. 'That won't be necessary.'

'I'd like to help, Byron,' she insisted, taking a pace towards him, and in the shaft of afternoon sunlight coming through the shop window her honey-gold hair assumed a touch of brilliance as it curled softly about her small oval face. 'Honestly I would,' she added persuasively.

'You're a very giving young woman, Megan.' Byron scowled down at his dusty boots. 'Frances was right when she said that one could so easily take advantage of your kindness and your generosity, and I'd hate to think I might fall into that category by taking your assistance for granted.'

'Don't be silly!' She laughed off his remark with a touch of embarrassment. 'And don't take everything my dear cousin says so seriously. Frances set herself up as my defender and protector when we were children, and I shall always adore her for it, but I know I have more gumption than she sometimes gives me credit for. I enjoy doing things for the people I care about, but I absolutely draw the line at becoming a willing, mindless slave.'

Byron nodded with understanding, but he was still frowning when he left the curio shop a few minutes later and walked off in the direction of his office which was situated across the spacious foyer of the main building.

Megan closed up shop some minutes later. It had been a tiring and frustrating day, but that did not stop her from making her usual detour down a dusty Land Rover trail to where a small, makeshift enclosure was now situated within the confines of the new veterinary building. She had had the enclosure erected a few months ago when she had taken on the task of fostering an orphaned duyker, and it was a task which had afforded her a great deal of satisfaction.

The young duyker gambolled towards Megan when she entered the enclosure. It was eager for the handful of wild grass which she always picked along the way, and the late afternoon sun lengthened their shadows across the earth when Megan went down on her haunches to speak to the animal in a lowered voice.

'It's almost time for you to move out and fend for yourself.'

The duyker stared back at her with those uncomprehending, soulful brown eyes while it munched delicately on the succulent grass, and the pain of parting tugged mercilessly at Megan's heart. She reached out with the desire to stroke the smooth, greyish-brown coat, but the small antelope darted aside with an inherent wariness which had not dimmed during the course of rearing the animal in captivity.

'You'll be OK,' Megan murmured reassuringly to the watchful duyker, but she knew that her reassuring statement had been directed mainly at herself.

Byron had warned that the most difficult part of fostering an orphaned animal was having to set it free into the wild, and Megan sighed as she rose from her crouched position to leave the enclosure. The duyker would soon have to be released to roam free in the game park. But not yet, she told herself with agonising reluctance. Not yet!

The familiar smell of the bush was all around her, and she drew it deeply into her lungs as she paused in her stride along the concrete path which led to her bungalow. Her appreciative glance strayed across the large hillside camp with its attractively thatched bungalows, recreational facilities and shady mopani trees. In the distance, silhouetted against the blue, cloudless horizon, she could see the baobab trees which had fascinated her since her arrival in the bushveld town of Louisville. Their branches looked like roots jutting into the sky and, as a child, she had promptly dubbed them 'upside-down trees'.

Megan laughed inwardly at herself. She was now a woman of twenty-four, and she felt far removed from that insecure ten-year-old orphan who had arrived in Louisville fourteen years ago. She had grown to love the South African bushveld and its people, and she was always impatient to return to her home when her illustrative work forced her to spend a few days in Johannesburg.

She had moved out of town to live with her cousin for a while on the farm, Thorndale, which Frances had purchased four years ago. Thorndale adjoined the game park, and Megan had enjoyed sharing the old stone homestead with her cousin, but it was time for her to move out when, less than a year after buying the farm, Frances married Byron Rockford. Both Byron and Frances had tried to persuade Megan to stay on, but she had been adamant. A bungalow which was within walking distance of her curio shop at Izilwane would be ideal, and Frances and Byron had finally agreed, knowing that she would be safe within the confines of the camp in the game park.

A smile of pleasure lifted the corners of Megan's soft mouth when she finally went into the one-bedroomed bungalow which was now her home. The curtains at the window matched the design of the woven rugs which lay scattered across the tiled floor in the small lounge, and she had added a few personal items to the customary cane and pine furnishings to give the bungalow a homely, lived-in appearance, but it was not the décor she was thinking about as she quickened her stride through the lounge into her bedroom. It had been a long and suffocatingly hot day, and she was eager for a shower and a change of clothing before she ventured into the kitchen to prepare dinner.

Half an hour later, refreshed and considerably cooler in a floral cotton skirt and white blouse, she was moving about efficiently in the small kitchen which Byron had had built on for her to make the bungalow more comfortable. She enjoyed cooking for herself in the evenings and seldom had a meal in the restaurant. It was a form of therapy, but on this particular evening she felt vaguely disturbed.

Her thoughts insisted on drifting back almost a year to that occasion when Revil Bradstone, chairman of Bradstone Promotions, had summoned her urgently to his offices in Johannesburg to commission her to do the illustrations for one of his company's many projects. It was during her week-long stay in the city that she had been invited to attend a function at Revil's home, and it was there that she had encountered the man who was to blame for the turbulent thoughts coursing through her mind.

Chad McAdam had been one of the many guests on that warm night who had spilled out on to the wide terrace from the Bradstones' spacious living-room. They had not been introduced, Megan had heard his name quite by chance, but for some obscure reason she had never entirely forgotten him. She had glimpsed him leaning nonchalantly against a pillar at the far end of the well-lit terrace, a drink in his hand and a stunning brunette hovering at his side, and she could remember thinking that he was the best-looking man she had ever set eyes on.

Megan had stared, she could not help it, and when he had looked her way, sensing her appraisal, she should have felt nothing stronger than mild embarrassment, but instead she had been mortified. His warm, assessing gaze had touched her with an arrogant intimacy that had made her blood clamour hotly through her veins in response, but just as swiftly he had subjected her to a cold, almost contemptuous stare.

Chilled and shaken to the core, she had seen his firm mouth curving in a cynical smile as if, in some uncanny way, he had been aware of every confusing emotion which had spiralled through her, and, after all this time, Megan still cringed inwardly when she recalled the stinging heat which had suffused her cheeks. She had left the Bradstone residence soon afterwards, determined to forget that brief encounter with Chad McAdam, and she thought she had succeeded. Until now!

The man who was taking up the position of resident veterinary surgeon at Izilwane could not possibly be the same cold-eyed, cynical-mouthed man she had met a year ago. That would be just too much of a coincidence, she told herself sternly, but she could not halt those tiny shivers of apprehension that were racing along her spine.

'Don't be an idiot, Megan O'Brien!' she reprimanded herself sternly while she added the diced potatoes and carrots to the meat stewing on the stove. 'You're jumping to conclusions, and that isn't like you at all!'

She somehow shrugged the matter aside, and channelled her thoughts in a positive direction. Now that the busy summer season was behind them she would have time to take an inventory of the stock in her shop. March through to May were always relatively quiet months, with the exception of the Easter holidays, and perhaps she would also have the opportunity to do the landscape painting which Frances had asked for so long ago.

It was seven-thirty that evening when Megan collected the key to the bungalow which had been allotted to the vet and, balancing the tray on one knee, she unlocked the door and went inside. The interior was spotless, she had seen to that personally, but she was filled with dismay when she went into the kitchen and flicked the light switch against the wall. One of the kitchen windows had been left open, and the cupboard tops were covered with a layer of dust after the freak wind which had ripped through Izilwane the day before.

Megan saw to the food she had brought across on the tray, then she set to work, wiping the surface of the kitchen cupboards and rinsing out the cloth in the water she had tapped into the sink beneath the window. She worked swiftly, in a hurry to get back to the sketches she had started after dinner, but she was wiping down the last cupboard when she heard a car door slamming, and the sound jarred her nerves.

She drained the sink hastily and wiped it while her glance darted anxiously at the door, considering it as a possible means of escape. It led out into a small, gated courtyard from where she could dart across to her own bungalow, but it was too late. She could hear footsteps in the lounge, and they were rapidly approaching the kitchen.

Megan had never before been nervous of meeting strangers, but for some peculiar reason her natural calm deserted her on this occasion when she realised that she was no longer alone. Her heart was beating wildly in her throat, almost suffocating her, and there was a visible tremor in her hands as she wrung out the cloth and draped it across the dish rack to dry.

She turned slowly, forcing a smile to her lips and desperately trying to compose herself, but her smile froze about her mouth as she faced the dark-haired man who had paused in the doorway leading from the lounge. He was casually dressed in a white, open-necked shirt and beige slacks, but her gaze shifted higher, and it was with a sense of renewed shock that she found herself looking into those cold, assessing grey eyes she remembered so well.

Tall, broad-shouldered and lean-hipped, Chad McAdam seemed to fill the kitchen with his daunting presence when he stepped forward, and Megan's insides were in the grip of an unfamiliar vice as she faced him with the width of the circular wooden table between them. He smiled cynically, and Megan once again had that odd conviction that he was aware of every damning thought and emotion that was flitting through her.

'I wasn't expecting a welcoming committee.' His voice was deep and well-modulated, but Megan detected a ring of mockery in its depths as he lessened the distance between them, and she could almost swear that the kitchen was shrinking in size with every step he took towards her.

'You weren't expected until much later,' she pointed out with an admirable show of outward calmness. 'I live next door and, since the restaurant staff are not on duty this evening, I offered to prepare a meal for you. You'll find it in the oven, and there's a fruit dessert along with a litre of fresh milk in the refrigerator. The tea and coffee canisters are in the corner cupboard if you would like to make yourself something to drink.'

There was something about this man's demeanour that awakened in Megan a strange and intense desire to turn and run. She had never felt awkward in anyone's company before, but Chad McAdam somehow had the ability to make her feel jittery and gauche.

'I believe one good turn usually deserves another,' he remarked scathingly. 'Were you hoping to share the meal you'd prepared, and then perhaps a little more as a reward?'

Megan was not accustomed to having her charitable actions misconstrued, and she stared up at him, convinced that she must look as stupid as she felt. What kind of woman did he think she was? she wondered distastefully when she managed to regain her composure.

'I had dinner almost two hours ago, and it wasn't my intention to hang around here and act as a welcoming committee when you arrived.' Her honesty was wasted on this man. There was cynical disbelief in those cold eyes raking her slender body from her honey-gold hair down to her sandalled feet, and she felt a little sick inside as she picked up the tray she had left on the table. 'Goodnight, Dr McAdam,' she added coolly, turning towards the door.

'Wait!' His imperious command halted her when she had gone no more than a few paces, and she turned warily to find him observing her intently with that hint of cynicism still curving his perfectly chiselled mouth. 'I pride myself on the fact that I seldom forget a face—especially a woman's face—and I'm convinced we've met somewhere before. What's your name?'

'It's Megan O'Brien,' she answered him stiffly, reluctant to prolong this confrontation.

'Ah, yes! You're the young lady from the curio shop with whom I shall be sharing a telephone line for a period of time.' His glance trailed over her with renewed interest, but that quizzical frown lingered between heavy eyebrows which were curved in a permanently cynical arch. 'Have we met before?'

Megan hesitated, not quite sure how to answer him. He was quite capable of mocking her for remembering if she told him where they had met before, but it would not take him long to discover that she had lied if she said something to the contrary. It seemed that, either way, she was bound to be mocked.

'We haven't exactly met before.' Her gaze did not waver from his, but it took an effort to sustain his piercing, probing glance. 'We were both guests at a function in Johannesburg which was hosted by Revil and Alexa Bradstone, and that was almost a year ago.'

'Yes, I remember now.' His smile deepened with that stinging mockery she had feared. 'You looked as if you were trying to hide among the potted plants at the other end of the terrace when I caught you staring, but when I looked for you afterwards you'd gone.'

'I left early.'

'Pity,' he murmured, his firm mouth twisting with derision. 'We shall, no doubt, be seeing each other quite frequently in future, and I shall look forward to every meeting, Megan O'Brien.'

Megan's powers of perception deserted her completely where Chad McAdam was concerned, and she left his bungalow in a hurry, too confused and bewildered to find a suitable response to his statement.

Paper crackled in her skirt pocket as she walked briskly through the moonlit darkness to her bungalow. It was the note she had intended leaving in his lounge to tell him about the meal she had left in the oven, and her fingers curled about it, crushing it into a tight ball in an unfamiliar display of anger.

Late that night, as she lay awake in bed listening to the night sounds, she was confronted by the renewed discovery that there was something about Chad McAdam which she had never encountered in anyone else before. It was dislike; a dislike so intense that it almost bordered on contempt. And it had been directed at *her*! *Why?* They were strangers, they knew nothing about each other, so what could she possibly have done that Chad McAdam should dislike her so actively?

Megan was in a disturbed frame of mind when she opened up her shop for business on the Friday morning. She had noticed a blue Porsche parked in the carport alongside Chad McAdam's bungalow, but there had fortunately been no sign of the man himself. An uneasy feeling had manifested itself in Megan since their meeting the previous evening, and she was unaccountably nervous and edgy when Jack Harriman entered the shop some minutes later.

Jack was a lean, wiry man in his mid-thirties, and Megan had seldom seen him when his sandy-coloured hair did not lie untidily across his lined forehead. He wore khaki like everyone else, but the epaulettes on his shoulders signified the rank of chief game warden, and she relaxed considerably when she looked into the smiling blue eyes of this man whose friendship she had come to value over the past five years.

'You're usually out with your patrols at this time of the morning,' she remarked, her glance teasing. 'Are you playing truant today?'

'I believe our resident vet has arrived,' he jolted her back on to that nervous tightrope she had been walking since the night before.

'He arrived last night,' Megan confirmed, and Jack's blue gaze sharpened with curiosity.

'Have you met him?' he asked, following her into her small office to the rear of the shop.

'We exchanged a few words.'

'What's he like?'

She shrugged with an affected casualness, and reached up to take a pile of stock sheets off the shelf above her desk. 'You'll have to decide that for yourself.'

'So it's like that, is it?' Jack laughed throatily.

'Like what?' she asked, schooling her expression before she dared to turn and face him.

'Our resident vet has failed to make a favourable impression on you,' he explained, his eyes twinkling with humour. 'That's it, isn't it?'

'First impressions can be deceiving,' she tried to rectify matters, and Jack's expression sobered a fraction.

'That's true,' he nodded, 'and your opinion of him might change once you get to know him.'

Megan could have told him that she had no desire to get to know Chad McAdam, but she remained silent. She confided in Jack about most things, but her unexpected meeting with Chad McAdam the previous evening was something she did not want to discuss with anyone until she had sorted out a few things in her own mind.

'I have to go,' Jack interrupted her thoughts. 'Byron has arranged a get-together in the committee room to welcome Dr McAdam, and if I don't leave now I'm going to be late.'

He strode out, leaving Megan in a ponderous mood which lasted until Dorothy, a sturdily built black woman, entered the shop. Dorothy had been Megan's assistant for the past three years, and in her presence Megan managed to put Chad McAdam out of her mind to start taking stock of the contents of the shop.

The post was delivered at ten-thirty each morning, and Megan and Dorothy were taking a welcome break with a cup of tea when a batch of letters was deposited on the glass display counter. Megan sifted through them idly, but one envelope in particular made her reach for her letter opener. She slit open the envelope, and her face lit up with excitement as she read the enclosed letter and examined the attached consignment note.

'I'll be back in a short while, Dorothy,' she told her assistant. 'There's something of importance I'd like to discuss with Mr Rockford.'

Megan's heart was beating hard against her ribs as she left her shop and walked across the slate-tiled, thatch-roofed foyer. A vague idea had taken shape in her mind when she had read that letter, but there was no sense in taking it beyond the 'idea' stage unless she knew she had Byron's approval.

'Come in, Megan,' he beckoned from behind his cluttered desk as he saw her hovering in the doorway. 'I have a mound of paperwork to get through before I drive Chad into Louisville to collect the Land Rover he had railed up from Johannesburg.'

'Perhaps this isn't the most opportune moment for the matter I want to discuss with you,' she smiled, quite prepared to shelve this conversation until it was more convenient for Byron.

'Goodness knows I need a break,' he growled with a glimmer of a smile in his tawny eyes as he flung his pen down and leaned back in his chair. 'Sit down and tell me what's on your mind.'

'I'm expecting the first consignment of fashionable safari-type outfits which I designed last year. I also designed the African motifs for the various garments, if you recall, so I'm naturally very excited about it, and I wondered if we might include a fashion show in the Easter holiday programme,' she explained hastily as she sat facing him across the width of his desk. 'It could be an outdoor event, perhaps around the pool area, and afterwards we could serve wine and snacks to enable the models to mingle among the guests to give them a closer look at the quality of the clothes.'

'That sounds like a perfectly good idea to me,' Byron agreed. 'Who do you have in mind to model the clothes?'

'I'm afraid I haven't given that side of it much thought,' Megan confessed with a touch of embarrassment. 'It might be a good idea to get in touch with Alexa Bradstone in Johannesburg, and, if I'm lucky, she might supply the models through her agency.'

'That would add a highly professional touch to this venture of yours,' he agreed gravely. 'Yes, I like the idea of a fashion show being included in the Easter programme, and I'd like to suggest that you speak to Bill

Hadley. If you explain to him what you have in mind, then he'll see to the catering side for you.'

Bill Hadley was Izilwane's entertainments manager, and Megan did not envisage any problems in that quarter. Bill was always very helpful and obliging when someone approached him with new suggestions for the entertainments section, and Megan's spirits were high when she finally returned to her shop.

She was impatient to contact Alexa, but when she picked up the telephone she discovered that Chad McAdam was busy on the line. More than an hour passed before the line was finally free, but she had barely dialled Alexa's number when she heard Chad McAdam lift the receiver in his office.

'Please cut your conversation short,' he instructed harshly when he realised that the line was in use. 'I have an important call to make.'

He replaced the receiver abruptly, leaving Megan stunned, and then a heated, unfamiliar fury rose within her. How dared he! How *dared* he instruct her to cut her conversation short when he had occupied the line for the past hour!

Megan was fuming inwardly, and she had to make a concerted effort to calm herself when Alexa Bradstone's soft, clear voice intruded on her angry thoughts.

'Alexa, it's Megan O'Brien.'

'What a marvellous surprise!' exclaimed Alexa. 'How are you, Megan?'

'I'm very well, thank you. Look, I haven't got much time,' Megan added hastily, 'but I have something in mind and I'm hoping you might be able to help me.'

She explained as swiftly as she could the reason for her call, and afterwards there was an agonising silence at the other end of the line while Alexa consulted her agency's diary.

'I happen to have a few models free over Easter, and they would be ideal for what you have in mind,' Alexa informed her after a few nail-biting seconds had passed.

'I might as well admit that I'm tempted to persuade Revil that we should accompany my models on this trip.'

'It would be wonderful to see you both again,' Megan admitted with an inward sigh of relief. 'I can't tell you how grateful I am that you're going to help me out with this venture.'

'Aren't you finished yet?' an impatient male voice cut in rudely on their conversation, and Megan's latent fury rose to a new level, but she somehow succeeded in controlling it.

'I'll be done in a minute,' she said abruptly, and there was a decisive click at the other end to indicate that he had slammed down the receiver.

'Who was that?' Alexa demanded curiously.

'Chad McAdam,' Megan almost spat out the name. 'He was one of the guests at that function I attended at your home a year ago, so you must know him.'

'Yes, of course,' said Alexa, 'but what's he doing up there at Izilwane?'

'He's been appointed resident veterinary surgeon, and until he gets his own private line he will, *unfortunately*, be sharing mine.'

'Oh.' There was an odd little silence before Alexa ended their conversation with a hasty, 'I'll be in touch, Megan, and please do be careful.'

Alexa's strange remark echoed repeatedly through Megan's mind. *Please do be careful!* Of what? Megan wondered, frowning as she replaced the receiver. Or should she ask of *whom*? Not knowing sent an unexpected shiver of fear racing along her spine, but she shrugged it off and went back to work. There was so much to do, and there was suddenly so little time to do it in that she dared not waste it on imaginary fears.

Megan and Dorothy were jotting down the items of hand-crafted pottery on display when Chad McAdam put in an unexpected appearance. His white shirt and slacks accentuated the tanned, muscular fitness of his body as he cast a brief, appreciative glance about him, and the fact that he had angered Megan earlier that morning was temporarily forgotten, but when those cold grey eyes met hers she felt a strange new tension spiralling through her.

'I'm getting a lift into Louisville with Byron,' he said curtly. 'Take a message if anyone calls, and leave it on my desk.'

He turned on his heel, and Megan stared incredulously at his broad back when he strode out of the shop, then she started to shake in a fit of uncontrollable indignation and anger.

'Who the *devil* does that man think he is!' she demanded of no one in particular, her blue eyes blazing with fury in her white face as she slammed her clipboard down on to the glass counter. 'He monopolises the telephone for most of the morning, and when at last I get a chance to phone, he rudely interrupts my conversation to order me off the line, then he walks in here and has the gall to instruct me to take messages for him as if I'm his—his *confounded* secretary!'

Dorothy's eyes widened like saucers in her dark face. 'I think you need a holiday, Miss Megan. You've been working too hard.'

Megan turned on her, that fierce light of battle still in her eyes, but she regained her control, drawing one deep, steadying breath after another in an effort to calm herself, and the angry tremors slowly subsided. *Nothing*, and *no one*, had ever succeeded in rousing her to such an intense level of anger, but Chad McAdam's arrogant behaviour somehow had the ability to trigger that hitherto hidden emotion inside her.

'I think you may be right, Dorothy.' She combed her fingers through her hair, ashamed of herself now that she had calmed down. 'Perhaps I do need a holiday, but there's so much to do now that the summer season has passed that I can't possibly contemplate going away.'

'You go home for the weekend and leave me to take care of everything,' suggested Dorothy, her seniority by fifteen years giving her the authority in this instance. 'Go home now, Miss Megan, and don't come back until Monday morning.'

Megan hesitated, but the suggestion that she spend the weekend at home with her parents in Louisville was tempting, and she finally succumbed to it, knowing that she could leave the shop in Dorothy's capable hands.

Her taut features relaxed and she smiled at her assistant. 'Remind me to increase your bonus at the end of this year, Dorothy.'

Megan left a few minutes later, and the midday heat enveloped her like a suffocating cloak when she stepped out of the air-conditioned building. The sun sat high in the fleckless sky, scorching the parched earth and creating a mirage in the shimmering distance amongst the acacia trees to indicate water where there was none.

It had been a long, hot summer with very little rain. The level of the dam in the game park had dropped considerably, and the bushveld heat had never been more oppressive, but the weather had not affected the tourist intake at Izilwane. The game park had lost none of its appeal as a holiday resort, and it had been filled to capacity during the Christmas holidays. The bungalows had been fully booked right through to the end of the summer season, and the Easter holidays still lay ahead of them, when the park nearly always drew a large crowd from the towns and cities.

Megan packed a weekend bag, and half an hour later the security guards at the main exit acknowledged her with a friendly salute as she drove past in her white Mazda.

CHAPTER TWO

THE ROAD to Louisville had been tarred with the advent of the game park. The trip took no more than fifteen minutes, and, as always, Megan knew a sense of peace when she arrived at the two-storeyed mansion where her parents lived. The autumn roses were flowering in the terraced garden, but she did not pause to admire them as she walked swiftly from the driveway towards the entrance of the house with its panelled glass windows on either side of the door.

Vivien O'Brien was speaking on the telephone in the hall when Megan walked into the house, and despite Megan's gesticulations that she should continue, her mother ended her conversation abruptly.

'What a lovely surprise, darling!' Vivien embraced Megan warmly. 'It's most unusual for you to arrive home at this early hour on a Friday.'

'Dorothy seemed to think I needed a break, so I left her in charge of the shop.'

'That woman is an absolute gem,' Vivien declared with grave sincerity. 'Have you had lunch?'

Megan shook her head and smiled up into her mother's dark eyes. 'No, I haven't, but I'm really not hungry.'

'Could I tempt you with a salad roll and a cup of tea?'

The smell of freshly baked rolls suddenly wafted towards Megan from the direction of the kitchen, and she relented. 'Consider me tempted.'

She left her bag in the hall and accompanied her mother into the kitchen to help with the buttering of the bread rolls while her mother prepared the salad filling and made the tea.

Her mother had aged well, Megan could not help thinking while she observed the tall, slender and elegantly dressed woman moving about in the large, modern kitchen. Vivien O'Brien was in her late fifties with barely a wrinkle on her striking features and a mere smattering of grey at the temples of her dark hair, which was brushed back in the casual but attractive chignon she always favoured. The dark eyes smiled easily, and always there was this feeling of genuine love and warmth emanating from the woman who, fourteen years ago, had taken Megan into her heart and her home.

'Byron popped in about an hour ago to deliver that crate of fresh vegetables Frances had promised me,' Vivien told Megan casually when they sat down to lunch in the dining-room. 'I also met Chad McAdam, and when we started chatting I realised that I'd known his father.'

Megan digested this information along with a mouthful of her salad roll. 'Did you really?' she asked warily.

'Trevor McAdam was a wealthy industrialist, and I met him for the first time about fifteen years ago,' Vivien elaborated with a frown creasing her smooth brow. 'He was a charming old man, but cynical and disillusioned, and it appears that Chad has inherited those characteristics from his father.'

Megan did not consider it necessary to add to her mother's shrewd observation that Chad McAdam could also be rude and arrogant. 'Is Trevor McAdam still alive?' she asked instead.

'No... poor soul.' Vivien sipped at her tea before she continued. 'He died four years ago and left behind a vast fortune which had to be divided equally between his two children. I understand that neither Chad nor his sister were actively involved in the business before their father died, but between the two of them they're now in possession of the controlling shares in the Aztec Corporation, and, according to Chad, he's now forced to divide his time between his chosen career as a vet and that of a boardroom director.'

Megan had heard of the Aztec Corporation. It was a vast organisation with tentacles reaching into almost every industry in the country, and she was somehow surprised to learn that Chad McAdam was in control of it. 'What about Chad's mother?' she asked curiously. 'Did you ever meet her?'

'Trevor McAdam had been a widower for a long time when I met him, so I imagine his wife must have died when Chad was still very young.'

Megan felt saddened by what she had been told, but she had come no closer to understanding the man whose face had haunted her periodically for so many months before he had walked back into her life with a vengeance.

That evening, after dinner, she told her parents about her plans for a fashion show at Izilwane during the Easter holidays. They discussed the subject in detail since Peter and Vivien O'Brien were always interested in their daughter's activities, and Megan was pleasantly tired when she finally went to bed.

It was after breakfast on the Saturday morning before Megan had the opportunity to take the flagstone path across the neatly trimmed lawn which led to the two-bedroomed cottage in the spacious grounds of her parents' home. It had been her intention to work on a watercolour painting of a pride of lions lazing in the shade of an acacia tree, but the paint dried on her brushes and the painting on the easel remained nowhere near to completion. She seldom thought about that time of her life before she had come to Louisville, but on this particular morning her mind persisted in raking up those unpleasant memories.

She had been on the back seat of the car when the collision had occurred. Both her parents had been killed, but she had escaped miraculously with concussion, minor lacerations and severe bruising. Dr Jessica Neal had tended to her physical as well as her mental wounds during her stay in a Johannesburg hospital, and a bond was established between them which was still there today.

After being discharged from hospital, and with no relatives to take a ten-year-old child into their home, Megan had been sent to an orphanage. Jessica Neal had promised to keep in touch, but a few weeks later she was offered a partnership with Doctors O'Brien and Trafford in Louisville. Megan had not looked forward to Jessica's departure from Johannesburg. She had believed they would never see each other again, but Jessica had surprised Megan by arranging for Megan to join her up in the northern Transvaal for the July school holidays. And this was where it had all begun, Megan was thinking as she cast a reminiscent glance about the light, airy studio which had once been Jessica's lounge.

Dr Jessica Neal had kept her promise after all, and that train journey to Louisville had been the start of a new life for Megan. She had moved into this very cottage with Jessica, and that was how she had met Dr Peter O'Brien and his wife, Vivien. A childless couple and an orphaned child; both needing to give and receive that special kind of love. Jessica had sensed their need; she had perhaps gambled on it, but she had triumphed in the end with the growing attachment between the O'Briens and Megan. The result was that Megan had never used the return ticket which would have taken her back to the orphanage in Johannesburg. Jessica, with the help of her influential father, had assisted Peter and Vivien to arrange a swift adoption, and Megan Leigh became Megan Leigh O'Brien.

'Am I interrupting something important?'

Megan's thoughts were dragged back to the present at the sound of that familiar voice, and she spun round on her stool to face her cousin, who was observing her quizzically from across the room.

'No, of course you're not interrupting anything, Frances,' she smiled at the tall young woman who had gathered her dark, shoulder-length hair into the nape of her neck with a hyacinth-blue scarf that matched the silky maternity dress she was wearing. 'What are you doing in town?' she asked, sliding off her stool to clean her brushes and pack them away.

'I had an appointment with Dr Jessica this morning,' Frances explained, lowering herself into an armchair without waiting for an invitation, and stretching her long, shapely legs out in front of her. 'She says I'm disgustingly healthy for a woman who's seven months pregnant.'

'I hope you're going to continue taking such good care of yourself to ensure that you and the baby stay that way,' Megan cautioned her, turning from her task to study her cousin intently.

Frances had always led a healthy, active life on the farm, and Megan was very much aware of the fact that her cousin could react impulsively and a little carelessly at times.

'You don't have to worry,' Frances laughed off Megan's obvious concern. 'I promised Byron at the start of my pregnancy that I'd confine myself to the Land Rover instead of a horse until after the baby's birth, and I intend to keep it that way.'

'I should jolly well think so!' agreed Megan, leaving her brushes to dry and lowering herself on to the stool which she had drawn close to Frances' chair. 'How is Dr Jessica?' she asked, her memories of the past still very much on her mind. 'Is she well?'

'She's well, and busy, as always, involving herself in the physical as well as the personal well-being of her patients.' Frances' dark eyes sparkled with affectionate humour, but her expression sobered the next instant. 'She asked about you and complained that she hasn't seen much of you lately.'

Guilt stabbed at Megan and she winced inwardly. 'These past months have been so hectic, but that's no excuse for not taking the time to pay her a visit.'

'Now that we're on the subject of visiting, it's been ages since the last time you spent some time with us out at Thorndale,' Frances voiced her own grievance. 'What about coming out to lunch tomorrow and spending the afternoon and the evening with us?'

'I'd like that, and thanks for the invitation.' Megan's agile, practical mind leapt on to further possibilities. 'I might also make use of the opportunity to saddle up a horse after lunch and take a ride down to the river to make a few preliminary sketches for that landscape you wanted.'

'I'll arrange to have a horse saddled and waiting for you after lunch tomorrow.'

Megan studied her cousin's striking features speculatively, and a faintly mocking smile played about her soft mouth. 'You're spoiling me, Frances, but I suspect that your generosity is prompted by your impatience for the landscape I promised you.'

'Naturally!' Frances' face was set in an unfamiliar, haughty mask, and Megan lapsed into a fit of giggles which coaxed a smile from her cousin. 'What's so funny?'

'You look exactly like my mother when she's in one of her reprimanding moods,' Megan explained at length, stifling her laughter behind her fingers and marvelling, not for the first time, at the family resemblance between Vivien O'Brien and her niece.

'That reminds me,' Frances remarked as she rose to her feet with a guilty start, 'Aunty Viv sent me to tell you she has tea and scones waiting in the living-room.'

'Then we'd better not keep her waiting,' Megan replied, getting up off her stool and removing the paint-spattered smock she had worn to protect her white cotton frock.

'By the way, have you met Dr McAdam?' Frances wanted to know when they walked across the smooth green lawn towards the house, and Megan stiffened, instantly on the defensive.

'I have, yes.'

'I met him very briefly last night when he came to Thorndale to discuss something with Byron, but I'm dying to know what you think of him,' Frances continued, unaware at that moment of the tension this topic of conversation had aroused in Megan.

'I don't know him well enough to risk an opinion.'

'You don't like him.' That was an intuitive statement, not a query, and Megan looked up to see Frances shaking her head in incredulous disbelief. 'Megan, this isn't like you at all. I've never known you to take an instant dislike to anyone.'

Megan looked away to avoid her cousin's probing, speculative glance. There was a closeness and an easy camaraderie between Frances and herself which had begun in their childhood, but in this particular instance Megan encountered an odd reluctance to share her thoughts and feelings with Frances.

'I don't dislike Dr McAdam,' she contradicted her cousin quietly but defensively. 'I simply find him incredibly annoying, and I think the less I see of him the better.'

'This sounds intriguing,' Frances remarked with a teasing note in her voice. 'I must say he's very good-looking, and I thought he was rather nice.'

Nice? Megan almost laughed out loud. There were several adjectives she could have conjured up on the spur of the moment to describe Chad McAdam, but *nice* had definitely not been one of them!

Thorndale & The Grove—F & B Rockford. That familiar sign was clearly visible as Megan approached the turn-off to the farm. The Grove lay directly beyond Thorndale, and both farms adjoined the Izilwane Game Park. It was for this reason that Byron Rockford had not hesitated three years ago when he had been offered the opportunity to purchase the Grove. The much-needed extension to the game park had been carried out with swiftness and care, but Byron had reserved a large portion of the land for himself and, with Frances' assistance, he was breeding a strain of Afrikaner cattle which was making the other ranchers in the district sit up and take notice.

Megan eased her foot off the accelerator and changed down to a lower gear as the old sandstone homestead on Thorndale emerged at the end of the long avenue of jacaranda trees. The thatch-roofed house had been enlarged considerably since Frances' marriage and, not wanting to deviate from the original structure, Byron had had sandstone carted on from a quarry near Louisville. The garden was still as colourful as always with its flamboyant trees, scarlet poinsettias, and amber to deep scarlet bougainvillaea which ranked profusely along a trellised section of the veranda.

A metallic blue Porsche was parked close to the house in the shade of an old jacaranda tree, and Megan felt an uncomfortable tightness gripping her insides as she pulled up behind it in her dusty white Mazda. What was Chad McAdam doing at Thorndale on this particular Sunday?

She was getting out of her car and slamming the door shut with a measure of irritation when Frances emerged from the house and walked towards her at that brisk, long-legged pace Megan knew so well. A worried frown was creasing Frances' smooth brow, and Megan could imagine the reason for it.

'You never told me Dr McAdam would also be joining us for lunch,' she accused, half in jest and half in earnest, when Frances reached her side.

'Byron invited him without my knowledge,' Frances explained, her dark gaze filled with concern. 'I'm sorry, Megan.'

'You don't have to apologise,' Megan assured her cousin with a calmness she was far from experiencing as she took a firm grip on her canvas shoulder-bag before accompanying her cousin across the sun-drenched garden towards the house. 'I know I said that the less I see of him the better, but that doesn't mean I intend to make life difficult for myself, or for everyone else, by turning tail every time Chad McAdam happens to be in the vicinity.'

'I'm glad to hear you say that,' Frances responded gravely in a lowered voice as they stepped on to the wide, shady veranda and entered the cool interior of the house.

Byron and Chad halted their conversation and rose politely from the comfortable depths of their armchairs as Frances ushered Megan into the spacious, airy living-room with its charming mixture of modern and antique furnishings.

'It's good to have you here again, Megan.' Byron's smile was warm and welcoming as always when he approached her, and, with the comforting weight of his arm about her slim shoulders, he turned her purposefully towards the man who stood observing them in speculative silence. 'I presume you've met Chad?'

'Yes, we've met,' Megan confirmed stiffly, meeting those cold grey eyes for the first time since entering the room, and she encountered once again that odd sense of shock at the suggestion of icy contempt in their depths.

His glance flicked dispassionately over her small, slender body in the blue summer frock before he inclined his head briefly in greeting, and an awkward silence seemed to hover in the room as Byron gestured Megan into a chair.

'I think Megan could do with a glass of wine before lunch,' Frances suggested, her voice sounding brittle in the silence as she lowered her weighty body into the chair beside Megan's and stretched her long, shapely legs out in front of her for comfort.

Byron's rugged features wore a grim expression, and his tawny gaze darted curiously from Chad to Megan, but he turned without speaking towards the ornately carved teak cabinet in the corner of the room. He poured Pinotage into a long-stemmed crystal glass and handed it to Megan, and she took a hasty sip of the crimson liquid in an attempt to steady her nerves while Byron topped up Chad's glass as well as his own.

Endless seconds seemed to pass before the conversation started to flow, but Megan did not participate in it unless she was spoken to directly, and at the luncheon table, an hour later, she was still content to remain a silent observer despite the curious glances Frances darted at her. She hoped to learn something while she listened to the inflections in their voices, and took mental note of the various, telling expressions that flitted across their faces, but Chad McAdam remained an enigma to her.

He was dressed casually in a burgundy-coloured shirt, blue denims, and blue and white canvas shoes. He looked outwardly relaxed seated across the table from her, but Megan was aware of every movement he made, and wondering at that inner tension she sensed in him which made her suspect that every muscle in his magnificently proportioned body was flexed for action.

There was something else which she happened to notice during the course of their meal. Frances' dealings with men during those years spent at an agricultural college had primed her for any situation, and Chad failed in his attempts to disarm her with his cynical, often contemptuous manner. Frances would bounce back every time with her usual straightforward sincerity, and Megan could almost swear she had seen a look of admiration flash across Chad's handsome face, but it was gone as swiftly as it had appeared, leaving her to think that she could only have imagined it.

'We've always had two veterinary surgeons in Louisville, but they have such a vast area to cope with that many farmers have often been deprived of their services,' Frances was saying when they had returned to the living-room with their coffee, and her statement was followed by Byron's deep-throated chuckle.

'That's a polite way of letting you know that you're going to be kept pretty busy dividing your services between the game park and the cattle ranchers in the district,' he told Chad.

'That's why I applied for this post.'

Chad's reply staggered Megan into wondering why a man like him would want to give the impression that he wished to bury himself in his work. Byron and Frances exchanged glances, obviously stunned into wondering the same thing, but Frances was the first to recover.

'More coffee, Chad?' she offered calmly, but he declined with a shake of his dark head, and it was at this point that Megan decided it was time she made her escape.

'I'd like to be excused, if you don't mind, Frances,' she said, aware of Chad's faintly cynical appraisal as she rose to place her empty cup in the tray. 'I want to change into something more comfortable and take that ride down to the river with my sketchbook and pencils.'

'What about you, Chad?' Byron suggested hospitably. 'I'm expecting a call some time this afternoon from a chap near Phalaborwa who might have a white lion for me, but I could have a horse saddled for you.'

Megan experienced a stab of alarm that threatened to choke her. If she had needed someone to accompany her on this ride, then Chad McAdam would have been the very last person she would have selected as a companion.

Chad's firm mouth twitched with a suggestion of a smile. 'The last time I sat astride a horse was four years ago, and I admit that I'm not an expert, but I wouldn't mind renewing the experience if Megan has no objections.'

His challenging statement focused everyone's attention on Megan, and she felt as if she had been driven into an uncomfortable corner with everyone waiting to see how she would react. A wave of resentment surged through her. This wasn't fair! There was only one way she could respond to Chad McAdam's challenge, and they all knew it!

'You're welcome to join me,' she heard herself saying with a calmness that belied the storm of protest inside her.

'That's settled, then,' nodded Byron, seemingly unaware of Megan's predicament as he rose to his feet and gestured that Chad should follow him. 'We'll meet you at the stables, Megan.'

Frances was frowning fiercely at her husband's departing figure as Megan picked up her canvas bag and left the living-room to walk briskly down the passage towards the guest-room which she always occupied when she stayed overnight at Thorndale.

She had learnt a long time ago to accept the things she could not change, and acceptance helped to restore her calm composure while she changed quickly into a yellow checked shirt and faded blue denims. She was pulling on her riding boots when there was a light tap on the bedroom door. The door opened before she could call out in response, and she looked up to see her tall, beautiful, but clearly agitated cousin entering the room.

Frances had something on her mind. Megan knew her cousin much too well not to sense her present mood, but Frances was strangely reticent as she watched Megan tugging at her boots until they fitted comfortably.

'Megan...' Frances seated herself beside Megan on the foot of the bed with its colourful patchwork quilt while Megan picked up her canvas bag and carefully checked the contents. 'I'm worried about you,' she said at length.

'I can take care of myself,' Megan assured her cousin with a faint sparkle of amusement lurking in her eyes. 'I could always use my pencils as a weapon if I should find myself in a position where I need to defend myself.'

Frances shuddered visibly while she stared wide-eyed at the viciously sharpened lead points of the assortment of pencils which Megan had produced from the interior of the canvas shoulder bag.

'I wasn't suggesting that you might be subjected to a physical assault,' she elaborated hastily. 'I'm sure Chad McAdam could charm a bone away from a dog if he wanted to, but I suspect he has ice instead of blood in his veins, and you're such a warm, gentle creature that I can't help being afraid for you.'

Megan agreed with her cousin, but only up to a certain point. She was convinced that Chad McAdam could be an extremely dangerous mixture of calculated charm, steel and ice which confused and bewildered her. He disturbed her intensely, and she would continue to be wary of his contempt until she was capable of understanding the reason behind it, but she did not fear him as a man.

'Frances, I adore you for your concern, but it really isn't necessary.' Megan was three years younger than her cousin, but at that moment she felt strangely older and wiser as she kissed Frances on her cheek and rose to her feet in one fluid, graceful movement. 'I'll see you later, and don't worry about me.'

Chad was mounting Stardust, the chestnut mare, when Megan arrived at the stables, and she had to admit to herself that he looked magnificent seated astride a horse. Byron was standing beside Juniper, the dapple-grey gelding which Megan favoured, and she avoided meeting Chad's narrowed glance as she shouldered her canvas bag and took the reins from Byron to lift herself into the saddle with the practised ease of an experienced rider.

'It's a scorching day, and I suggest you use the trees for cover on your way down to the river,' Byron warned her.

'I'll do that,' she promised.

She did not wait for Chad. She dug her heels lightly into Juniper's sides and urged him on into a brisk gallop past the camps where Frances' Brahman stud cattle were grazing.

The sun was stinging her face and arms and, taking Byron's advice, she headed towards the shelter of the gum and poplar trees on the ridge directly ahead of them. Chad caught up with her seconds later, and she cast a brief glance in his direction to notice that he sat remarkably well in the saddle for a man who claimed he was not an expert. She risked yet another glance at him, the artist in her revelling in the perfect symmetry of his attractively sculpted features, and she was admiring his stern profile with the straight, high-bridged nose and strong, jutting jaw when his grey glance collided unexpectedly with hers.

A wave of embarrassing heat surged into her cheeks at the knowledge that she had been caught staring in much the same way she had stared a year ago, and she leaned forward in the saddle, the wind whipping through her short, honey-gold curls as she urged Juniper on to a faster speed. The dapple-grey gelding responded instantly to her silent command, but it was not the exhilaration of the ride that heightened the colour in her cheeks. It was that stinging mockery she had glimpsed in Chad's eyes before she had wrenched her glance from his, and she cursed herself silently for allowing him to make her feel and behave like a gauche teenager.

She slowed Juniper down to a comfortable trot when they finally reached the tall, shady trees which grew so abundantly from the crest of the ridge down to where the fast-moving river wound its way among rock-capped hills through Thorndale property, and Chad followed her example.

The familiar pungent smell of the bush mingled with that of horseflesh and leather, and Megan began to relax in the saddle, her small, fine-boned body moving in perfect unison with the rhythm of the animal beneath her. They rode in silence through the dappled sunlight, neither of them making an attempt at conversation, but Chad was not a man to be ignored. He had the ability to make his presence felt, and Megan was uncomfortably aware of him with every fibre of her being as she took the lead along the path that veered left down to the river.

The river was still flowing strongly despite the fact that the bushveld had not had sufficient rain during the summer months, and birds chirped and fluttered noisily in the trees where they had sought safety in building their nests high along the willow branches trailing across the water.

Megan and Chad had dismounted and were tethering their horses to a sturdy acacia tree when Chad broke the silence between them. 'I had grave doubts that someone as slightly built as you could control an animal of Juniper's strength and size, but you ride well.'

'Frances taught me to ride when we were children, and she's one of the best.' Megan did not hesitate to give credit where it was due, and she smiled inwardly at the memory of those riding lessons so long ago as she eased her canvas bag off her shoulders and studied her surroundings from an artist's point of view.

'You obviously admire your cousin a great deal.'

'I do,' she confessed abruptly, aware of a trace of cynicism in his voice, but doing her best to ignore it as she walked away from him to seat herself in a shady spot on the uprooted stem of an old tree.

'You didn't want me to come along on this ride, did you,' he stated with an unexpectedness that wrung an honest response from Megan.

'No, I didn't.' She took her sketchbook out of the canvas bag and looked up suddenly to find him observing her intently through lowered lids with his thumbs hooked into the leather belt hugging his denims to his lean hips. 'I'm sorry if that sounds rude,' she added contritely, 'but it's the truth.'

'Are you sulking because I've neglected to thank you properly for the meal you prepared for me the other night?' he demanded, smiling derisively, and Megan stiffened with indignation.

'I am not in the habit of sulking, Dr McAdam, and leaving a home-cooked meal in the oven for you had been intended as a gesture of good-neighbourliness for which I didn't expect to be thanked,' she informed him, the chilling displeasure in her voice reflected in her eyes as she met and sustained his piercing glance. 'That's the way we are in these parts, generous and neighbourly, and in time you might learn to view our actions with less suspicion.'

His sensuous lower lip thinned and his mouth became twisted with cynicism. 'It's my experience that a woman's generosity is meted only according to what she expects in return.'

Chad's distorted opinion of women shook Megan considerably, but it also afforded her a glimmer of understanding which made the corners of her taut, angry mouth relax and quiver with the effort to suppress a smile.

'Do you find that amusing?' he demanded curtly, his eyes narrowed to unfathomable slits, and she felt compelled to explain.

'I was under the impression that your dislike was directed at me *personally*, but I realise now that you don't have a very high opinion of women in general, and I must confess to a feeling of relief.' She stared up at him thoughtfully, studying the rigid contours of his good-looking features and wishing she could probe beneath that harsh, cynical mask. 'I don't suppose,' she added speculatively, 'that you allow your opinion to deprive you of female company.'

'Women can be entertaining as long as a man doesn't take them seriously, and they do happen to serve a purpose.'

His implication was as clear as the sexual undertone in his deep, velvety voice, and his sensuous mouth curved with derisive mockery as she felt embarrassment staining her cheeks a deep pink.

'I'll take a stroll farther up along the river and leave you to your sketches,' he ended their conversation abruptly, and he was walking away from her before she had time to recover sufficiently to formulate a suitable reply to a statement which she knew had been intended to shock her.

Megan stared after him until the denseness of the trees along the banks of the winding river obscured him from her vision, and then her embarrassment slowly gave way to an intense sadness. Life could be cruel at times, and she could only think that it must have dealt Chad McAdam a savage blow. It had robbed him of the ability to care, and it had left him with the misguided notion that women were playthings that served a purpose only in a man's bed.

A beetle landed on her opened sketchbook with a thud that startled her out of her reverie, and she sighed as she flicked it off and reached into her canvas bag to select one of her pencils. She worked steadily, her pencil moving with rapid, confident strokes across the paper, but she could not rid her mind entirely of the conversation she had had with Chad.

A woman's generosity is meted only according to what she expects in return, he had said, and Megan shuddered inwardly as she recalled the contempt in his voice. She had lived a reasonably sheltered life as a member of a close-knit family, moving among people who were warm-hearted, loving and generous to a fault, but she was no longer an innocent child who had to be sheltered from the sometimes harsh realities of life. She was aware that there were many women who fitted Chad's description aptly; women who gave very little in return for what they had received, but it was wrong of him to believe that all women were like that. So terribly wrong!

Megan could not be sure how long she had sat there working, but the rocky-ridged hill, the rippling river, and the trees along the opposite embankment had been reproduced on paper before her, and she was reasonably satisfied with the result. Her back felt stiff, and she was arching it to ease the tension in her muscles when a twig snapped behind her, startling her into an awareness that she was no longer alone.

'That's very good,' Chad announced himself, stepping over the log and gesturing to the sketchbook on her lap as he seated himself beside her.

He smelled of the sun and a woody cologne. It was a potent mixture that tugged at her senses and heightened her awareness of him as a man in a way that alarmed her considerably.

'This is merely a preliminary sketch for a painting,' she explained self-consciously as he leaned towards her to take a closer look at her work, and her nerves seemed to become alerted to something which she failed to put a name to when his arm brushed lightly against hers.

'This may only be a preliminary sketch, but you've already succeeded admirably in capturing the essence of your subject on paper.' The compliment was unexpected, and when he raised his glance to subject her to a speculative stare, Megan lowered her gold-tipped lashes to hide her confusion, but instead she found herself staring in strange fascination at the fine dark hair springing from his tanned, sinewy forearm. 'I believe you've been remarkably successful in business as well as in the arts, and that's quite an achievement for someone so young,' he added, increasing that odd tension inside her when she looked up to meet that relentless, probing glance. 'You project an image of youthful innocence which could be deceiving, so what are you, Megan O'Brien? Eighteen? Nineteen, perhaps?'

'Twenty-four,' she replied, averting her gaze to focus her attention on the hawk which had been circling the sky for some time.

'Impossible!'

'It is, nevertheless, a fact,' she laughed nervously, arching her aching back once again and altering her position slightly to avoid contact with that long, muscular thigh which had shifted so close to her own. 'How old are *you*, Dr McAdam? Or am I not supposed to ask?'

His cynical mouth twitched with the suggestion of a smile when she glanced at him. 'Add nine years on to your age.'

She raised her finely-arched eyebrows in a mocking response. 'Thirty-three? Impossible! You don't look a day older than...'

'Careful, Megan,' he warned softly, his mocking, compelling glance holding hers relentlessly, and she had to steel herself not to flinch away from those long, sensitive fingers tracing the line from her cheekbones down to her small, pointed chin. 'You happen to be treading on dangerous ground.'

That was true! His touch was like fire against her skin, quickening her pulse and underlining the fact that she would be treading on dangerous ground if she allowed herself to get too close to this man who was beginning to intrigue her to the extent that she felt an urgent need to know more about him. Common sense warned that Chad McAdam could disrupt the calm, comfortable existence she had carved for herself, and if she wanted to avoid being hurt then it would be safer to stay away. *Far* away!

Megan emerged from her thoughts to hear the horses moving about restlessly, and she retreated hastily behind that protective barrier of aloofness which she had erected earlier that day when she had arrived at Thorndale to find Chad there.

'I think it's time we returned to the house.' She rose abruptly to escape the tantalising caress of Chad's fingers before they could stray too far along her throat and busied herself packing away her equipment. 'The light has altered,' she offered as an excuse, 'and I could do with something cool to drink.'

Chad did not contradict her, but Megan was agonisingly aware of his silent mockery as they mounted their horses moments later and rode back to Thorndale's homestead at a leisurely trot. He knew that his touch had disturbed her, and she could almost hate him for reading her so accurately.

CHAPTER THREE

'YOU'RE NOT going to spend the night out at Izilwane,' Frances argued with Megan after dinner that Sunday evening when they left the dining-room to drink their coffee out on the veranda. 'You're staying here.'

'It's kind of you to suggest that I stay, but I——'

'I insist!' Frances interrupted, settling herself comfortably on the cane bench beside Byron. 'This is the first time in weeks that you've come to the farm, and you can't leave until we've had a decent conversation.'

'You're bossy,' Megan accused with mock severity.

'I know,' Frances agreed with a smile in her voice. 'Will you stay the night?'

Megan relented with a sigh. 'How can I say no when you ask so nicely?'

'I have a couple of important phone calls to make, so I'll leave the two of you alone,' announced Byron, rising to his feet and putting his empty cup in the tray on the low table before he went into the house.

Megan and Frances remained seated in the moonlit darkness, listening to Byron's heavy footsteps crossing the hall and growing fainter down the passage until there was a silence which was disturbed only by the screeching of insects in the undergrowth.

'This is quite like old times, isn't it,' remarked Frances, her reminiscent observation finally ending the companionable silence between them.

'Yes, it is,' Megan agreed on a sigh, recalling the many evenings they had spent together out on the veranda, relaxing after a busy day.

'I wish you'd find someone nice and settle down with a home of your own. Isn't there a chance that you and Jack——'

'Jack Harriman and I have never been more than friends, and that's the way it will always be between us,' Megan interrupted her cousin firmly. 'I'm in no hurry to be married, Frances,' she added for good measure, 'and I'm quite content with my life as it is at the moment.'

'Yes, I know you're happy and content in what you're doing, but one day you'll meet someone, and then you'll suddenly wake up to the knowledge that it isn't enough.'

Megan smiled into the darkness. 'I imagine that's true.'

'What happened this afternoon when you rode out to the river?' Frances changed the subject abruptly, and Megan was instantly on her guard.

'Nothing happened,' she replied evasively. 'Dr McAdam went for a long walk along the river while I made the preliminary sketch for the landscape you've been waiting for so patiently.'

'Is that all?'

Megan frowned at her cousin's shadowy figure seated on the cane bench, then her sense of humour rose to the fore and she laughed softly into the darkness. 'You sound disappointed. Were you hoping I'd say he tried to seduce me under the willows?'

'Certainly not, Megan!' her cousin responded indignantly. 'You must have talked, though, because I did notice that the tension had eased a little between the two of you when you returned from your ride.'

'He's a very cynical and embittered man,' Megan remarked thoughtfully. 'Someone must have hurt him very badly once, and he's neither forgiven nor forgotten.'

'You must have indulged in quite a revealing conversation,' observed Frances drily, and Megan was glad of the darkness as she felt her cheeks grow warm.

'Chad McAdam is a very difficult man to understand.'

'Most men are difficult to understand until you discover what it is that makes them the way they are.' Frances spoke with the wisdom of a woman who had experienced this for herself, and she was silent for some time before she added unexpectedly, 'Chad McAdam is a very attractive man, with his own fair share of idiosyncrasies.'

'So I noticed,' Megan laughed wryly.

'Don't get involved, Megan.'

A jackal howled in the distance as if to stress the urgency of Frances' warning, and the hair rose on Megan's arms. 'I don't intend to,' she stated firmly, suppressing a shiver.

'I'm glad to hear that,' Frances sighed audibly into the darkness. 'I'd hate to see you hurt.'

Their conversation ended there when Byron rejoined them out on the veranda, and later, when they went to bed, Frances' warning echoed repeatedly through Megan's mind before she went to sleep.

Don't get involved!

She did not want to get involved, but there was this cynical little voice at the back of her mind which persisted in saying that she might not have a choice in the matter.

The time had come for the duyker to be released into its natural environment. Megan knew she could no longer postpone it, and she was preparing herself emotionally for what she had to do when Chad emerged from the veterinary building on the Monday afternoon and saw her with the small antelope she had reared.

'The duyker has to go,' he instructed, approaching the small enclosure with a look of icy disapproval in his pale grey eyes. 'If you prolong this confinement the animal won't learn how to fend for itself.'

'I know,' she said, resenting his interference as she rose from her haunches to confront him. 'I was thinking of speaking to Jack Harriman this evening and making the necessary arrangements.'

Chad accepted her statement with a curt nod before he strode off in the direction of his bungalow, and Megan knew a strange desire to hurl something at that broad, departing back. He was a callous brute, and she doubted if he had ever had to let go of something or someone he had learned to care for.

Megan was up before dawn on the Tuesday morning. The bushveld air was cool and fresh, and the dew-wet earth sparkled in the watery rays of the sun as it rose slowly beyond the mountains in the distance. Birds twittered noisily in the mopani trees, and somewhere a dove was calling to its mate, heralding the awakening of a new day, but the magic of this moment escaped Megan as she coaxed the duyker into the small cage in which it was to be transported into the game park.

A handful of succulent grass was all she needed to accomplish this task. The duyker quivered nervously when the cage door slid into position, trapping it, and Megan thought her heart would break when those soulful brown eyes met hers for one brief second before Jack Harriman instructed his men to lift the cage on to the truck. Her throat ached, and she was fighting desperately to hold back the tears when she felt Jack's arm slide about her shoulders.

'He'll adapt very quickly,' he assured her, and she turned her face into his comforting shoulder.

'I know he will.'

She lifted her head a moment later as if someone had tugged her by the hair and, looking over Jack's shoulder, she saw Chad's khaki-clad figure walking towards them on his way to the veterinary building which housed his office, surgery and laboratory. He greeted everyone in passing, but his cold eyes skimmed over Megan with a hint of mockery in their depths, and her cheeks flamed. She had no reason to feel embarrassed and awkward about being seen with Jack, but suddenly she did, and she resented Chad for making her feel that way.

Moments later she was watching the truck disappear down the road with its cargo which had become so precious to her. She turned, her eyes misting with tears, and at that moment she saw Chad observing her from his office window with his features set in an inscrutable mask. What was he thinking? Was he enjoying her misery? Megan did not stop to wonder. She pulled herself together instantly and hurried back to her bungalow to exchange her denims and shirt for a cool cotton frock before she opened up shop.

She had very little leisure time during the ensuing weeks, and, with Dorothy's assistance, she had completed the laborious task of listing every item in the shop. New stock had been ordered and had arrived in time for the Easter holidays, but the shelves and glass counters had also been replenished with wood-sculpted ornaments, clay pots and colourful beadwork with a distinctive African flavour. The latter had been supplied by the very artistic team of local native men and women who, with Megan's encouragement, had long ago found a lucrative outlet for their work through her curio shop.

The first batch of safari outfits bearing Megan's designer label, MEGS, had arrived, and she had received notification that a second batch was on its way. The arrangements for the fashion show had also gone ahead smoothly, and the bungalows in the camp were filling up rapidly with visitors.

Megan caught only brief glimpses of Chad McAdam during those busy weeks before Easter, and when she did happen to bump into him, his manner had been cold and distant. On several occasions she had had to accept messages from farmers in the district requiring Chad's services as a vet, but, to her relief, he was in demand to such an extent that he had seldom been in his office when she had gone there to leave the messages on his desk.

She had decided sensibly that it would be safer to stay out of Chad's way, and pressure of work had made it possible for her to accomplish this, but that did not stop her thinking and wondering about him.

'He's a bit too abrupt and aloof for everyone's liking, but no one can deny that he's a damn good vet,' Jack had expressed his opinion one evening when he had dropped in to have a cup of coffee with Megan in her bungalow, and Megan had seen no reason to contradict that statement.

She was aware of the fact that Chad worked long, hard hours during the day, but she did not mention this to Jack Harriman, and neither did she mention that Chad seldom extinguished the lights in his bungalow before midnight. It would not do to give the impression that she was interested in the comings and goings of the veterinary surgeon, but, to be honest with herself, she *was*. She could not help it. The man intrigued her, and, despite her efforts to the contrary, she had caught herself on several occasions listening for his step, or searching the grounds in the hope of catching a glimpse of him.

She was kept busy in her shop until long after eight the Wednesday evening before Alexa Bradstone was expected to arrive at Izilwane with her models. This was an important occasion for Megan, and she had spent the hours carefully selecting the garments and the accessories which were to be modelled at the fashion show. She was thrusting a pile of letters and invoices into a folder when she turned to see Chad McAdam dwarfing the entrance to the small room which she used as an office, shrinking it to cupboard size, and her heart leapt nervously in her breast as she stared at his tall, khaki-clad frame.

'You don't usually work this late, do you, Megan?'

He took a pace into the office, adding claustrophobia to the many thoughts and feelings surging through her, and it felt as if an eternity passed before she managed to regain her composure sufficiently to answer him.

'No, I don't usually work this late, but there's still so much to do, and I want to be ready tomorrow when Alexa arrives with her models.' He was standing close enough for her to catch the faint but pleasing scent of his masculine cologne, and a strange weakness assailed her limbs. 'Was there something you wanted?' she asked, wishing he would state his business and go.

His appraising glance shifted from her lime-green blouse down to the tailored white slacks hugging the gentle curve of her hips and thighs, then he smiled twistedly. 'I was passing when I saw that the lights were still on, and I wondered if the shop was being burgled.'

Megan knew she would be a fool to believe him. There was something about him that made her feel edgy, but she could not decide what it was.

'I doubt that a burglar would have switched on the lights to advertise his presence, do you?' she mocked him, and his eyes observed her with a strange intensity as she turned from him to pick up her keys and the folder she had stuffed so full of papers.

'Are you locking up for the night?'

'Yes.'

She had answered him with an abruptness which had stemmed from her intense awareness of him as a virile, sensually attractive man. She wished he would leave, but he stood aside for her to precede him out of the office, and he lingered until she had switched off the lights and locked up the shop.

'I'll walk with you,' he announced unexpectedly when they left the building and stepped out into the cool night air to walk along the path leading towards their bungalows.

Megan resigned herself to the inevitable, but his silent presence beside her in the moonlight unnerved her, and her heart skipped a frightened beat as he accompanied her all the way to her bungalow. They ascended the shallow steps on to the small *stoep* at the entrance, and she unlocked the door, her hand fumbling when she switched on the inside lights before turning to face him.

'Goodnight, Dr McAdam,' she said warily, and her wariness intensified when he observed her with a gleam of mockery in his eyes.

'I was hoping you'd be neighbourly and invite me in for a cup of coffee.'

Megan gestured with the brown folder she had been holding up against her breasts like a shield. 'I still have a lot of paperwork to get through this evening, and I——'

'Don't make excuses, Megan,' he cut in accusingly, his hand gripping her arm and sending a thousand little shock waves darting through her as he propelled her inside and closed the door.

Megan was unaccustomed to being treated in this manner, and she shifted the bulky folder on to her hip to wrench her arm free of his disturbing clasp. 'Well, *really*!' she began indignantly. 'You have no right to——'

'It isn't going to work, you know,' he interrupted her once again, his deep, velvety voice touching her and confusing her.

'What are you talking about? What isn't going to work?'

Chad's narrowed gaze rested for a moment on the glossy, honey-gold hair curling softly about her delicate features, then it shifted lower to linger where the thrust of her breasts was clearly visible beneath the silk of her blouse. Megan felt a rush of blood surging into that part of her anatomy, and her cheeks were flaming when he raised his sensuous glance to that tiny pulse beating erratically at the base of her throat.

'There's no sense in denying that we've both been doing our best to avoid each other these past weeks,' he explained his confusing statement. 'There's an awareness between us which I'm sure you find as unacceptable as

I do, but by avoiding each other we've simply intensified it.'

Megan's breath seemed to lock in her throat. It was true! In her efforts to avoid Chad she had succeeded only in making herself more aware of him, but there was no joy in the knowledge that he felt the same about her. He had confessed that the only use he had for a woman was in his bed, and she had no intention of becoming involved with someone like Chad McAdam who would use her solely as an instrument with which to satisfy his physical urges.

'You're mistaken,' she contradicted him coldly, turning away from his disturbing nearness to deposit the bulky folder on the small writing desk beneath the window where the curtain billowed gently in the breeze.

'Am I, Megan?' he mocked her, foiling her attempt to put a safe distance between them by coming up behind her, and the warmth of his hands on her shoulders sent unfamiliar but receptive tremors racing across her nerve-ends. 'Something flared between us the first time we saw each other at Revil Bradstone's house party. I ignored it, but the reason for my abominable behaviour when I arrived here at Izilwane to find you in my kitchen was that I was shattered to discover that the feeling was still there.'

Megan could echo almost everything he was saying, but she dared not let him know it. 'Dr McAdam, you don't——'

'Chad,' he corrected, his breath stirring the hair against her temple and sending delicious little tremors racing along her spine. 'Call me Chad.'

'Chad,' she murmured obligingly, her body stiffening beneath those strong fingers moving against her shoulders in a deliberate caress which was beginning to affect more than her pulse rate. 'You're imagining things,' she added in a voice that was husky and unfamiliar to her own ears.

'I don't believe I am.' There was mockery in his soft, throaty laughter when he spun her round to face him, and her heart fluttered like a wild bird trapped in a cage as she met his probing, stabbing glance. 'Can you look at me, Megan, and tell me honestly that you don't feel anything?'

It was not in Megan's nature to lie. She had always told the truth no matter what the consequences, but she did not relish the outcome in a situation such as this. It was true that Chad had captured her interest long ago with no more than a brief glance across a crowded terrace, and it was also true that, since his arrival at Izilwane, he had awakened her to the most disturbing feelings, but her logical mind warned that it would be fatal to admit it.

'You're the best-looking man I've ever seen.' Her voice was admirably calm in the face of her own vulnerability as she confessed to a harmless truth in preparation for the abominable lie which necessity dictated would have to follow, but she dared not look into his eyes while she did so, and she concentrated instead on the strong line of his square jaw. 'You have good features—features I would like to sketch some day, but that's all it is, and I apologise if I've made you believe differently.'

His grip tightened on her slim shoulders, his fingers biting painfully into the tender flesh he had caressed only moments earlier. 'Why don't you want to admit the truth?'

'This is a ridiculous conversation!' she protested, fear making her resort to anger as her only defence. She avoided his rapier-sharp eyes, and brushed off his hands to back a pace away from him. 'I have a mound of paperwork to wade through this evening, and I don't wish to appear rude, but I'd appreciate it if you would leave now.'

'I'll go, Megan,' he assured her harshly, his fingers snaking about her arm when she would have turned away from him, 'but there's one question I would like to ask. Is Jack Harriman your lover?'

She drew an angry, indignant breath. 'That's none of your business!'

'I'm *making* it my business! Is he your lover?'

'*No*, he is *not!*'

'Then what's preventing you from admitting the truth?'

'Nothing and no one is preventing me from doing *any*thing!' she argued fiercely. 'You have no right to question me like this, and I insist that we discontinue this conversation!'

'You're right! There's been too much talk and too little action!'

Anger glittered in the eyes blazing down into hers, but the warning in their depths escaped Megan while she tried to cope with her rising panic, and she was totally unprepared when Chad jerked her up against him. He held her with her arms pinned helplessly at her sides, and the shock of finding herself caught up against his hard chest and muscled thighs seemed to electrify every nerve and sinew in her body. Her lips parted on a cry of protest, and he chose that moment to claim her soft, untutored mouth with an intimacy that made the blood flow at a hot, dizzying pace through her veins.

Megan was aware of her breasts hurting against the hard wall of his chest, and the tautness of his muscled thighs against her own. She wanted to voice her displeasure at this physical assault, but the firm, sensual pressure of Chad's mouth on hers stifled the sound in her throat, and then, to her dismay, a clamouring response rose from somewhere deep within her. It took control of her actions, robbing her of the ability to think rationally, and, her latent senses delighting in the hard warmth of his male body against her own, she relaxed in his arms and slid her hands up between them until her fingers met at the nape of his neck and lost themselves in the springy softness of his dark hair.

What am I doing? she asked herself in a brief moment of sanity, but Chad's tongue invaded her mouth, probing gently, and she promptly forgot to question the logic of her actions as she surrendered herself to a barrage of new sensations.

Chad's hands were roaming her body, their heat through the thin barrier of her clothes exciting her beyond measure, and she was unaware that he had unbuttoned her blouse until she felt the front catch of her lacy bra give way beneath his fingers, but she was somehow powerless to prevent those strong, sensitive hands from cupping her breasts. No man had ever been allowed to come close enough to touch her like this, and Chad's probing, caressing fingers against her taut nipples awakened a longing so intense that she trembled violently with the force of it.

'You might as well admit it, Megan,' he murmured against her mouth before he trailed a path of fiery kisses along the sensitive cord of her throat and across one creamy, exposed shoulder. 'What we feel for each other is more than just a casual interest.'

His words penetrated her drugged mind, alerting her to the chilling reality of what he had accomplished, and she came to her senses with a sickening start.

'*No!*' she cried out hoarsely, pushing herself away from him in dismay and dragging the front panels of her blouse together to cover her nakedness as she stood swaying in the aftermath of her plunge from that dizzy, ecstatic height into the stark pit of sanity. 'No, you're wrong!'

'Your lips may deny it, but your body can't lie, Megan,' he contradicted her with a derisive smile.

Her heart was having difficulty resuming its normal pace, and her breathing felt restricted, but along with her sanity came the humiliating knowledge that, while proving her a liar most effectively, Chad had succeeded in remaining emotionally unaffected by what had occurred between them.

Her cheeks flamed, and, having witnessed her humiliation, Chad wished her an abrupt, angry goodnight before he turned on his heel and strode out of her bungalow. He did not slam the door behind him, he closed it with the same amount of control he had exercised on his emotions, but the sound of the latch clicking into place jarred her raw, quivering nerves, and she flinched visibly.

She felt shattered, and she sat down heavily on the nearest chair as her trembling legs threatened to fold beneath her. Her throat tightened painfully and she was on the verge of tears, but with it came the crazy desire to laugh. Her emotions were bordering on hysteria, and, recognising the symptoms, she stifled the feeling forcibly to stare ashen-faced at the colourful woven rug beneath her sandalled feet. Her shame was a living, stabbing thing inside her, and she had a feeling that Chad was never going to let her forget her humiliating surrender.

Megan awoke the following morning with a throbbing headache that drove her out of bed at dawn in search of the box of aspirins she stored away in the bathroom cupboard. She swallowed down two tablets with water, and she was leaning weakly against the hand basin when her glance focused on her image in the mirror. Her eyes were heavy-lidded with deep shadows beneath them, and her face looked pale and pinched in the dawn light which filtered in through the frosted panes of the bathroom window.

'You look a mess, Megan Leigh O'Brien,' she told her mirror image with a grimace, and then the memory of what had occurred washed over her with all its shame and humiliation.

It was the emotional devastation of the night before which was now so clearly etched on her face, and she pressed her fingers against her pounding temples as she turned from the mirror with an agonising groan on her lips.

She had worked late in an attempt to shut out everything except the information in the documents she had had spread out on the desk before her, but she had not succeeded entirely. It had been after midnight before she had dragged herself off to bed, but she had lain awake in the silent darkness of her room, unable to forget what had happened, and failing dismally in her attempts to justify her own behaviour.

Chad's kisses had been an intimate invasion, his touch a profound delight, and her denials had been swept aside ruthlessly when her emotions had flared into something which she had been incapable of controlling. That was what Chad had wanted; to prove her a liar when she had denied her awareness of him as a man, and it was partly her failure to resist him which had left her tossing restlessly in her bed and cringing inwardly at the taunting memory of her surrender, but exhaustion had finally claimed her during those last few hours before dawn.

Megan opened the taps in the shower and slipped the satiny straps of her nightgown off her shoulders. It slithered along her body to the tiled floor, and she left it there to step into the shower cubicle. She stood for several minutes simply enjoying the relaxing sensation of that jet of tepid water pummelling her body. It was therapeutic, and her headache eased slowly along with the aching tension in her muscles.

She had a long, busy day ahead of her, and she had to erase thoughts of Chad McAdam from her mind if she wanted to cope with her work, she lectured herself firmly an hour later when she had breakfasted and was slipping into a blue cotton frock with shoestring shoulder-straps. Alexa Bradstone was expected to arrive at ten that morning with the models from her agency in Johannesburg, and Megan would need to summon every scrap of concentration while they carried out the final preparations for the fashion show, which had been planned for the day after Good Friday.

She applied her make-up a little heavier than usual, but she failed in her attempt to disguise the evidence of her restless night, and the clock on her bedside cupboard warned that she no longer had time to linger over it.

Doves were cooing high up in the mopani trees when she finally left her bungalow, and the neatly-trimmed lawns sparkled with dew in the slanted rays of the early morning sun, but Megan barely noticed. Her steps faltered momentarily when she drew near to Chad's bungalow, but she walked on again at a quickened pace. The curtains were drawn across the windows, but that did not necessarily signify that he was still there. He often rose at dawn to spend an hour or more in the laboratory, and...!

Oh, lord! she groaned inwardly. I know too much about his habits for someone who pretended not to notice!

It was a quarter to ten that morning when Megan heard the drone of an aircraft approaching the Izilwane landing strip. Alexa was a stickler for punctuality. She had said they would be arriving at ten and, as usual, they would be right on time. Fifteen minutes later the game park's ten-seater bus was driving up to the front entrance of the main building, and Megan was there with Bill Hadley, the entertainments manager, to welcome them.

Alexa Bradstone was the first to alight from the bus, and one's interest was instantly captured by that look of cool elegance and sophistication. Her silky, ash-blonde hair was piled casually on to her head, and her tall, slender body was sheathed in beige slacks with a matching top and a blue silk scarf draped skilfully about her throat to match her incredible eyes. Alexa was an extraordinarily beautiful woman, but Megan had discovered long ago that her beauty was not limited to her outward appearance, as some people imagined.

'Alexa!' Megan stepped forward, and they embraced each other warmly. 'Welcome to Izilwane.'

'It's good to be here.' Alexa was smiling broadly as she shifted her fashionable sunglasses higher on to her head and raised her flawless features to the sun to draw the air deeply and audibly into her lungs. 'Just to smell this tangy bushveld air is enough to revitalise me!'

Revil Bradstone stepped off the bus with a grey, light-weight jacket draped across one arm. He was tall and distinguished despite his casual attire, and the expression on Megan's face ignited a glitter of amusement in the grey eyes that were narrowed against the glare of the sun.

'Hello, Megan,' he greeted her with a hint of friendly mockery in his smile when he reached Alexa's side. 'Surprised to see me?'

'Surprised and delighted, Revil,' she replied, smiling up at the man who had set her on the road to success with her illustrations, and, ignoring the fact that he was the autocratic chairman of Bradstone Promotions, she reached up to plant a welcoming kiss on his lean cheek. 'I'm so glad you managed to accompany Alexa,' she added with her usual sincerity.

'Izilwane will always be a special place for us, and I was determined that nothing was going to stop me accompanying my wife on this trip,' he replied, placing a casual but faintly possessive arm about Alexa's waist, and husband and wife exchanged a glance which, Megan suspected, shut out the rest of the world for a brief moment.

'Ladies and gentlemen!' Bill Hadley raised his voice above the excited chatter of the two lean, clean-cut young men and four leggy girls who now stood grouped together beside the bus. 'I imagine you'd first want to freshen up after your flight,' Bill continued when he had gained their attention. 'The staff are awaiting you at reception, and from there you'll be shown to your respective bungalows, but I hope you'll all join us a little later at the pool area, where we have refreshments laid on for you.'

This news was greeted with an enthusiastic cheer from the group of six models Alexa had selected for this assignment, and they followed eagerly when Bill Hadley turned to lead the way towards the reception area.

'Where's Byron?' Revil questioned Megan as she accompanied them into the air-conditioned interior of the main building.

'Byron has been out in the game park since early this morning with Dr McAdam and Jack Harriman,' she explained, a shadow flitting across her sensitive features when she thought of Chad. 'I don't know what the problem is, but Byron radioed in a short while ago to say that Dr McAdam was collecting a few samples for analysis and that we could expect them back within the hour.'

She imagined Chad would be spending most of the day in the laboratory if he was collecting samples for analysis, and she could only hope that she was correct in this assumption. She felt awkward about having to face him again, and she prayed that, with added time at her disposal, she would be sufficiently composed during their next encounter.

'I'll see Byron later, then,' Revil was saying, and Megan hastily brushed aside her troubled thoughts when she felt Alexa's hand on her arm.

'You'll be joining us later for refreshments up at the pool, won't you, Megan?'

'I'll be there,' Megan assured Alexa when they reached the entrance to her curio shop, 'and Bill Hadley said he'd be free this afternoon to assist us with the final details for the fashion show.'

Alexa nodded and followed her husband across the spacious foyer towards the reception area, while Megan went off to her shop where Dorothy was attending to the purchases of a handful of customers.

'There was a telephone call for Dr McAdam,' Dorothy told her when they were alone. 'It was a woman, but she wouldn't leave her name and telephone number when I told her that the doctor wasn't in his office.'

Megan felt her stomach muscles contract in a nervous spasm. 'Did she leave a message?'

Dorothy nodded her turbaned head and handed Megan a small sheet of paper. 'She said to tell him she would call again at four this afternoon.'

'Please see to it that Dr McAdam receives this message,' Megan instructed, thrusting the piece of paper back at Dorothy as if it was burning her fingers.

Who was this woman who would not leave her name and telephone number where she could be reached? Could it have been Chad's sister? Or was she one of the many women with whom he had amused himself in the past?

Megan did not have time at her disposal to dwell on this subject, but it plagued her at odd moments during the course of the day. It was none of her business, she kept telling herself, but she could not help being curious.

CHAPTER FOUR

THE PREPARATIONS for the fashion show were halted on Good Friday, and Megan chose to spend a leisurely day with her parents in Louisville rather than remain in the camp. It was good to get away, to relax with her family, and it was late that afternoon before she drove back to Izilwane.

The sun was a fiery orb hovering on the western horizon as she parked her Mazda beside her bungalow, and there was a stillness in the air as if nature itself was settling down for the night. A flock of hadeda ibis flew low overhead to roost, their raucous call, ha-ha-ha-dahah, rending the silence, and Megan paused to observe their flight as she stepped from the carport.

A slight breeze stirred the skirt of her cotton frock about her legs and lifted the fine tendrils of hair at her temples, but it was going to be a beautiful night. There were children playing tag across the lawns, their laughter drifting clearly on the silence, and Megan smiled, remembering her own happy childhood in Louisville as she turned to go indoors.

She was rounding the corner of her bungalow when she stopped short, her calmness almost deserting her completely at the sight of Chad leaning against one of the wooden pillars on her *stoep* with his hands thrust deep into the pockets of his grey slacks and his blue shirt unbuttoned almost to his waist. Megan stared at him, torn between the pull of his magnetism and the frantic desire to run, and she was seriously considering the latter when he forestalled her.

'You can't walk away and pretend I'm not here, Megan,' he warned, gauging her feelings in that uncanny way of his, and she stiffened with resentment.

'I wasn't going to,' she almost snapped at him as she set her limbs in motion and climbed the shallow steps on to the *stoep*, but her heart leapt nervously into her throat when Chad pushed himself away from the pillar to lessen the distance between them.

'The temptation to walk away was there, wasn't it?' he mocked her, and she lowered her gaze as guilt sent a wave of heat rushing into her cheeks.

'Yes, it was.'

'I appreciate your honesty in this instance.'

She risked an upward glance to find him observing her with that cynical, almost contemptuous expression on his lean face, and a new wave of resentment surged through her to leave in its wake an aching, unfamiliar tightness about her heart.

'What do you want with me, Chad?' she sighed, lowering her gaze hastily as she felt the sting of tears against her eyelids and taking her key out of her handbag in the hope that he would take it as a hint that she wanted him to go.

'I want the pleasure of your company at dinner this evening.'

Several alarming possibilities had flashed through her mind, but a formal invitation to dinner had not been one of them, and she almost laughed out loud at herself when she inserted the key in the lock and turned it decisively.

'It's kind of you to invite me,' she said politely, pushing open her door, 'but I've a busy day ahead of me tomorrow, and I would like to have an early night.'

'You have nothing to fear, you know,' he mocked her, his hand coming down heavily on her shoulder to prevent her from entering her bungalow, and her nerves leapt at his touch as he turned her to face him. 'We'll be dining in the restaurant, Megan, and I'm not in the habit of molesting women in public places.'

'No,' she agreed caustically, remembering the last time they had been alone together. 'Only in private.'

He dropped his hand to his side and smiled twistedly. 'If I'm provoked, yes.'

Megan blushed profusely and cursed herself in silence as she averted her gaze to escape the mockery in his eyes. It had been foolish of her to draw attention to what had occurred between them during their last embarrassing encounter, but she regained her composure swiftly to meet his silent appraisal with a proud tilt of her head. Wouldn't she be tempting the devil if she had dinner with him? she wondered.

'Are you willing to risk it?' he asked intuitively, his glance trailing over her sensitive features and fastening on to that gleam of defiance in her expressive blue eyes.

'Is there a risk involved?' she counter-questioned with a touch of wariness, and his smile deepened with that familiar, stabbing cynicism.

'There's always the risk that you might enjoy yourself.'

'I suppose there is that possibility,' she agreed, tempted against her will, and Chad's glance sharpened on that unwilling smile plucking at the corners of her soft mouth.

'Do I sense a "yes" hovering somewhere behind that statement?'

'You're very persuasive, but . . .' She hesitated, refusal hovering on the verge of her logical mind, but it was acceptance that finally spilled from her treacherous lips in a shaky, 'Y-Yes.'

'Good!' he said abruptly with a hateful gleam of triumph in his steely eyes. 'Be ready at seven-thirty,' he added. 'I have a table booked, and you have my word that I shan't keep you out late.'

Megan stared after him until he entered his bungalow, and she had a nasty feeling that she was stepping foolishly into unknown and dangerous territory, but it was too late now to change her mind.

The restaurant was filled to capacity that Friday evening with visitors who had come from all over southern Africa to spend the Easter holidays in the game park. The log-cabin décor with its low-hanging lights like old-fashioned lanterns created a friendly, relaxed atmosphere, and diners were seldom encouraged to dress in anything other than casual attire.

Alexa and Revil Bradstone were seated at a table in a secluded corner. Megan had noticed them when she had entered the restaurant with Chad, and she had also glimpsed a fleeting look of concern on Alexa's face when they had greeted each other, but it was forgotten in the process of ordering a meal.

'Shall we drink to an enjoyable evening?' Chad suggested, raising his glass of wine to Megan when the steward had left their table, and the soft lighting had a mellowing effect on the harsh angles and planes of his striking features.

'Yes, I'll drink to that.'

She raised her glass to his before she brought it to her lips to take a steadying sip of the dry white wine she always preferred. She did not think that she would be nervous seated across the table from Chad in a crowded restaurant, but she was. She was aware of him in every possible way; aware of the beige lightweight jacket which accentuated the width of his powerful shoulders, and aware of that aura of masculine charm which was having such a devastating effect on her pulse-rate.

She tried to focus her attention on her drink, on the buzz of conversation around them, on anything and anyone other than Chad, but she looked up eventually as if her eyes had been drawn by a magnet to find him observing her quizzically across the small, square table. Why was he looking at her like that? she wondered, and then she realised that he was expecting her to reply to something he had said.

'I'm sorry, you were saying?' she rushed into speech, guilt staining her cheeks a deep pink as she gestured apologetically.

'I was asking you why you don't have your meals here in the restaurant.'

His eyes mocked and chastised her simultaneously for her inattentiveness, and she could feel that embarrassing warmth deepening in her cheeks. 'I like to prepare a meal for myself in the evenings,' she explained. 'It helps me to relax and unwind after a busy day.'

His glance trailed over her, taking in the sheen of the honey-gold hair framing her fine-boned features, and the creamy smoothness of her shoulders beneath the pencil-thin straps of her amber-coloured dress, but a nervous little pulse fluttered wildly at the base of her throat as his eyes lingered for an unnecessary length of time where the thrust of her small, firm breasts was clearly visible beneath the silky folds of her dress. It felt as if his eyes were scorching her through the material, touching her, and her body responded in the most embarrassing way.

'You're a very attractive young woman, Megan.'

'No, I'm not!' she brushed off his statement with a nervous laugh to ease that strange tension between them. 'My eyes are too big, my nose is too small, and I would have liked to be a couple of centimetres taller.'

'Don't underrate your physical appeal, but, now that you mention it, you certainly appear to be the odd one out in a family of tall people. You may have fair hair and blue eyes like your father, but that's where the resemblance ends.' Chad's stern mouth twitched with the first real sign of amusement. 'Are you a throwback or something?'

'Or something,' she replied, smiling at his faintly bewildered expression while she sipped at her wine, and she could feel herself relaxing as she explained. 'I'm not a blood relative, Chad. Vivien and Peter O'Brien adopted me when I was ten.'

His dark brows drew together in a frown above his narrowed eyes. 'No one has mentioned this to me before.'

'No one would.' Megan was not sure why she had confided in him, but his reaction amused her. 'I was accepted into the family fourteen years ago, and that has always been that.'

The waiter appeared at their table with their food, and that particular conversation was shelved, but Megan had not quite finished the grilled sole and spicy rice she had ordered when she looked up to find Chad observing her intently.

'Tell me more about yourself, Megan,' he ordered, using his fork to spear the last morsel of steak on his plate and popping it into his mouth.

'There's nothing much to tell.'

'Maybe not,' he agreed readily, 'but you can't tell me you're adopted and then leave me to wonder about your own parents.'

'There was a car accident,' she told him reluctantly. 'I sustained a few injuries, but both my parents were killed.'

She knew somehow that Chad would not be satisfied until he had heard it all, and she went on to explain briefly what had led up to that holiday in Louisville which had given rise to her adoption.

'You must have been a very unhappy little girl,' he commented with an unfamiliar gravity in his voice when she lapsed into silence.

'I was unhappy after the accident and during that brief stay in the orphanage, but these past fourteen years have been the happiest years of my life.' She lapsed into a contemplative silence and was surprised to discover how much she had actually told him about herself. 'The history of my life isn't a subject I'm in the habit of selecting as a topic for conversation, and I can't think why I'm discussing it with someone I barely know,' she added, vaguely annoyed with herself.

'We're no longer strangers, Megan.'

Chad's compelling glance drew hers across the candlelit table, and her heart skipped a nervous beat, but the waiter chose that moment to return to their table, and he created a welcome diversion while he removed their empty plates and served their coffee.

'I believe it's your turn to tell me about yourself,' Megan prompted when they were alone again. 'Did you have a happy childhood?'

'I imagine I did.' The smile curving his mouth did not reach his eyes. 'Children are adaptable to change.'

'It depends on what they have to adapt to,' she argued gently, sensing an undercurrent of bitterness in his flippant remark.

She watched him in silence while he swallowed down a mouthful of black coffee, and she was wondering whether she was going to be left in ignorance when he leaned back in his chair and smiled that twisted, mirthless smile which was beginning to tug at her compassionate heart.

'I was four years old when my mother ran out on us. She went to South America with her lover, and she died there a few months later when their small aircraft crashed into the Andes.' His voice was dispassionate, like an announcer reading the news, but the clenching and unclenching of his hand on the table was a visible contradiction. 'My father never married again, and I can understand why. Women are fickle where their emotions are concerned, and if a man wants loyalty and commitment he would do better to get himself a dog. Women can ruin a man unless he stays one jump ahead of them, and I vowed a long time ago that no woman would be given the opportunity to make of me the emotional wreck my father used to be.'

Megan felt as if she had been kicked in the stomach. His tone of voice had sharpened with icy contempt, chilling her and sending an involuntary shiver through her. 'I'm well aware of the fact that there are women who possess the characteristics you've mentioned,' she tried to reason calmly, 'but not all women are like that.'

'I have yet to meet a woman who isn't.'

Chad was once again the cold-eyed, cynical-mouthed man she had seen a year ago across the length of Alexa Bradstone's terrace, and it was clear that his opinion of women had been nurtured since childhood. Any bridges Megan might attempt to build would simply lead to nowhere, and knowing that there was nothing she could say, or do, to prove him wrong filled her with a disquieting helplessness.

She sipped at her coffee and switched to a subject which she hoped would inject a more pleasant note into their conversation, 'I believe you have a sister.'

'That's correct.' His expression hardened unexpectedly, and his eyes were narrowed to slits that flickered with anger in the flame of the candle between them. 'Matty is two years my senior, and she's yet another prime example of emotional instability in women. She's been married and divorced three times, and at the present moment she's living with a man of whom, she tells me, she's already tiring.'

Dear heaven! Megan thought despairingly. It's no wonder he has such a disgusting opinion of women!

'Perhaps your sister has simply been unfortunate in her choice of men,' she suggested charitably, but Chad's short bark of cynical laughter dispelled her theory.

'I'm more inclined to think that the men were unfortunate in choosing Matty, and I mentioned something to that effect when she phoned me yesterday afternoon.'

He had, without realising it, assuaged Megan's curiosity about the woman who had called the day before, but at the same time she recoiled inwardly from his statement.

'Have I shocked you?' he questioned her as if he had sensed her withdrawal, and she shook her head.

'I think you and your sister must be two very unhappy people, and I feel sorry for you.'

'I don't need your pity, Megan.' His face was a forbidding mask as he glanced at the slim gold watch strapped to his lean wrist and signalled the waiter. 'It's ten-thirty, and you wanted to have an early night.'

Megan's mind was in an unhappy turmoil when they left the restaurant a few minutes later, but the night air washed over her, cool and refreshing, and she tried to relax in the blessed silence of the bushveld which was disturbed only by the chirping of the crickets in the undergrowth.

She had angered Chad, she knew that, but his anger seemed to desert him as swiftly as it had risen when they walked along the path which led to their bungalows. They did not speak, nor did Chad make an attempt to touch her, but there was a subtle change in the atmosphere between them which was making her intensely aware of his tall, muscular presence beside her. It was odd, but it was as if every part of her body had suddenly been alerted to his maleness, and this strong physical attraction between them unnerved her. The woman in her had never responded like this to any other man before, and...please God...she did not want to waste her feelings on a man like Chad McAdam.

She had left the reading lamp switched on in her lounge, and Chad stood directly in the shaft of dim light that shone out on to the *stoep* through the parting between the partially drawn curtains. His eyes glittered with something suspiciously close to laughter when he took her key from her to unlock the door, and Megan had a horrible suspicion that he had cut in on her thoughts in much the same way he so often cut in on her telephone calls.

'Are you going to invite me in?' he asked, and she was still searching for a polite way to say 'no' when his hand in the hollow of her back propelled her inside.

Don't panic! she warned herself, feeling as if Chad had isolated them from the rest of the world as she heard him close the door behind them. She had felt safe with him in the restaurant, but to be alone with him like this was quite a different matter. She had been alone with him before in this very room, and...!

'I must thank you for a pleasant evening,' she said, thrusting aside the memory of the havoc he had created with her emotions, and trying desperately to appear calm and natural, but her voice sounded as awkward as she felt at that moment.

'I'm glad you enjoyed it.'

Megan turned her back on his smiling appraisal to put her evening purse down on the low, circular table. Her mind was searching frantically for something to say which would ease this odd tension in the air between them, but the words seemed to remain lodged in her throat when she turned to face him again.

His eyes were lit with a strange fire, and they were raking a slow, sensual path down the length of her slender body, lingering on the hollows and soft mounds that stamped her a woman until she had the curious sensation that she was standing naked before him.

'Don't look at me like that!' she rebuked him, her heart beating so hard and fast in her throat that her voice sounded choked.

'I think you have a beautiful body,' he smiled sensuously.

'*Stop it!*' she hissed furiously, walking away from him, but he was beside her in an instant, his hands on her shoulders spinning her round to face him.

'You're blushing,' he murmured incredulously, raising one hand to brush the back of his fingers against her flaming cheeks.

'I don't know why that should surprise you,' she retorted stiffly, his touch igniting a new kind of fire inside her.

'I thought blushing was a forgotten art.'

Her blue gaze held his accusingly. 'You say that as if you think it's a *practised* art!'

'Isn't it, Megan?' he demanded cynically, his fingers trailing lightly across her throat, seeking and finding sensitive areas which, until then, she had not known existed and sending little shivers of pleasure cascading through her. 'Isn't it all part of that game of sexual intrigue between a man and a woman?'

'I don't know what you're talking about,' she replied, trying to ignore the sensations he was arousing by focusing her attention on the collar opening of his white shirt, but it did not help her much when she found herself staring at the start of that dark mat of hair on his chest.

'Don't pretend with me, Megan,' he laughed harshly, releasing her, and allowing her to breathe a little easier. 'The game you're playing is familiar to me, I've played it too often not to recognise it, but you're playing it by a complete new set of rules, and I admit that I'm intrigued.'

Megan was convinced that she must look as confused as she felt at that moment, but through the mist of her confusion came the knowledge that Chad was blind to everything except his own arrogant convictions.

'I don't play games, Chad,' she assured him with a calmness she was not experiencing at that moment. 'I don't play games, but I do try to pattern my life according to a certain set of rules, of which honesty is the most important.'

'You weren't honest with me the other night.'

'No, I wasn't,' she admitted readily, lowering herself into a chair when her legs threatened to cave in beneath her and clasping her hands nervously in her lap. 'I was afraid to admit the truth, and I acted out of character in a moment of panic.'

'What were you afraid of?'

'I was afraid of you, but mainly I was afraid for myself,' she confessed, watching him through lowered lashes as he seated himself in a chair close to hers and stretched his long legs out in front of him. 'I've never met anyone like you before,' she added with inherent honesty, 'and I'm finding it rather overwhelming.'

Chad's eyes were stabbing chips of steel beneath the sardonic lift of his eyebrows. 'Would you care to clarify that statement?'

'Do I really have to spell it out for you?'

'I would appreciate it.'

Megan's insides were knotting with anxiety, and she wished she had had the good sense to keep her mouth shut, but it was too late now.

'I admit that, from the first moment I saw you, there's been an undeniable attraction—an awareness—if you like, but I'm also repelled by your contemptuous opinion of women,' she explained, her colour deepening, and her glance wavering from his to settle for a moment on her tightly clenched hands in her lap. 'I'd like to spend more time with you to get to know you, but I also consider that unwise when I think of where it might eventually lead.'

'It can only lead to a better understanding between us, and what's wrong with that?'

Chad's mockery did not escape her, and anger rose like a hot tide inside her which she had difficulty in suppressing. It was obvious that he wanted to make this as awkward as possible for her, but she was equally determined to bring one very important matter to his attention. Her heart was beating out a nervous tattoo against her ribs, but her expression was controlled and her glance was cool when it met his.

'By your own admission you have only one use for a woman, and that's in your bed, but I'm not going to bed with you, Chad,' she said quietly. 'Not now, and not in the foreseeable future.'

He observed her in silence for a moment, his eyes narrowed and piercingly intent, then he smiled derisively. 'This is certainly a new angle, but I think I might enjoy the novelty of a chase.'

'You simply don't understand, do you?' She rose agitatedly to her feet and walked a few paces away from him before she turned to look at him with a spark of helpless anger in her wide blue eyes. 'It's totally inconceivable to you that there could be women in this world who need to love and know that they're loved in return before they'll go to bed with a man.'

'*Love!*' His lips curled back in a snarl against sharp, white teeth. 'Love is a disease of the mind, Megan, and if you're weak enough to succumb to it, then it makes you vulnerable to whatever pain the object of your love wishes to inflict upon you.'

'Love is a two-way commitment, Chad. It involves fidelity and trust, and——'

'Fidelity! Trust!' His expression was contemptuous as he drew in his feet and stood up. 'To expect those two qualities from a woman would be as foolish as to come between a hungry lion and its prey.'

If Megan had not been so angry she might have sensed the underlying bitterness to his scathing remarks, but her compassionate nature was stunted in this instance by a strong desire to shake him physically.

'I really do feel sorry for you, Chad,' she said coldly, facing him across the width of the small coffee-table with her hands clenched so tightly at her sides that her nails bit painfully into her soft palms. 'You've incarcerated yourself behind an impenetrable barrier of misguided notions. You've shut yourself off emotionally, allowing life itself to pass you by, but take care that you don't wake up years from now to the discovery that you can add loneliness to your long list of grievances.'

'That's a very pretty speech.' He applauded her mockingly as he stepped around the table towards her. 'You forget, however, that while there's money in the bank there'll always be women who'll be willing enough to sell themselves in order to get their slice.'

'You're speaking to the wrong customer, Chad,' she retorted distastefully. 'I don't need a slice of your bank balance, and I can't be bought.'

'Life has taught me that everyone has their price.' His mouth was curved in that twisted, cynical smile she hated so much, and, taking her unexpectedly but firmly by the wrists, he applied a tugging pressure that made her stagger up against his hard body. 'What's yours, sweet Megan?'

She stiffened against him, his body heat and the clean male smell of him an assault on her senses that left her temporarily without the power of speech, but it was anger that finally loosened her tongue.

'Find someone else!' she instructed coldly, making a futile attempt to free herself from those steely fingers while she stared up at him with eyes that were stormy with the mixture of unfamiliar emotions stirring inside her. 'Find someone who'll play your game of sexual intrigue to the rules you're accustomed to, and leave me out of it in future!'

'It's too late for that.' Chad lowered his head to hers, but in turning her face away to avoid his kiss she exposed her throat, and his warm mouth trailed fire across her sensitive skin, arousing a spate of unwanted sensations which seemed to snatch her breath away. 'The more I see you, the more I want you, and I know that, given the opportunity, I could make you want me too.'

His tongue sought and found the sensitive hollow behind her ear, and the shivers of pleasure cascading through her made her realise just how vulnerable she actually was. It was a shattering discovery, and one which she was determined to keep to herself.

'No, I could never want——'

'Don't deny it, Megan,' he interrupted her throatily, nibbling at her earlobe before his mouth shifted lower to that little pulse which was beating so wildly at the base of her throat. 'Be honest with yourself, and with me, by admitting that it's true.'

His fingers had slackened their punishing grip on her wrists, giving her the opportunity to jerk herself free, and she backed a few hasty paces away from him, but there was no escape from the burning intensity of those pale, probing eyes. They were making a mockery of her denial while that erratic pulse at the base of her throat was making it only too obvious that she was not physically immune.

'Oh, yes, Megan, I could make you want me as much as I want you at this moment,' he repeated, his gaze resting on the agitated rise and fall of her breasts beneath the soft silk of her evening dress. 'I know you're finding this difficult to accept under the present circumstances, but at some future date I'm going to take a great delight in proving it to you.'

His confidence frightened her into immobility, and she stared at him, her facial muscles as achingly rigid as her body when he raised his fingers to his forehead in a mocking salute and left.

Megan was not sure whether it had taken minutes or hours before she became aware of the fact that she was shaking from head to foot as if she had a raging fever. She was shaking to such an extent that her teeth were chattering, and she sat down heavily in a chair, wrapping her arms about herself until she could control the tremors, but she could not stop the frantic thoughts racing through her mind.

It was true! There was no sense in denying to herself that the feelings Chad had aroused in her were the first stirrings of desire. She had never experienced anything like this before, and it drove her into a state of panic knowing that she could have these strong physical yearnings for a man whom she was not even sure she liked.

'What am I going to do?' she cried out aloud, but the only answer she received was that of an owl hooting eerily into the stillness of the night.

The fashion show the following day was a resounding success which rocketed Megan's sales and left her with a batch of orders for more. The models were still mingling with the guests on the green, sloping lawn surrounding the pool when Megan and Alexa helped themselves to a glass of wine and a snack. They sought refuge from the afternoon sun beneath a thatched shelter and, sinking wearily into vacant chairs, they quietly congratulated each other on their joint effort.

'I'm so relieved that it all went off so smoothly,' Megan sighed, catching sight of her parents chatting to Bryon and Frances where Bill Hadley's staff were discreetly clearing away the ramp which they had erected for the fashion show.

'The credit is yours for all the hard work and planning you'd put into it before the time.' Alexa smiled at Megan over the rim of her long-stemmed glass. 'I could do with someone like you in Johannesburg.'

'Are you offering me a job?' Megan demanded with amusement dancing in her eyes, and Alexa shook her head ruefully.

'I could never offer you the scope you have here for your creative abilities, but I do need an assistant who would be capable of taking over the reins when I'm not there,' she explained in her soft, clear voice. 'I'm twenty-six, Megan, and I can't afford to wait much longer to have the children both Revil and I want so badly, but that means I shall have to find someone to take most of the work load off my shoulders, or I might be faced with the unpleasant task of having to sell the modelling agency.'

'You'll find someone suitable, I'm sure.'

'I think that's one of the things I like most about you, Megan. You're always so reassuringly positive.' Alexa's smile faded a moment later, and there was an unmistakable flicker of concern in her eyes as her glance met Megan's. 'You're one of the nicest people I know. You're loyal, sincere, and trusting, and you always give so generously of yourself. Don't let anything—or anyone—ever change you.'

Alexa was being subtle, but Megan did not need to be psychic to know that her relationship with Chad formed the basis of Alexa's concern, and it was not simply curiosity that spurred Megan to make use of this opportunity in an attempt to find out more about this man who had disturbed her so intensely since their first meeting.

'How well do you know Chad McAdam?' she questioned Alexa, holding her breath in anticipation, but a veiled look shifted across Alexa's expressive face.

'He's one of Bradstone Promotions' most valued clients,' she replied, being deliberately evasive, and amusement lifted the corners of Megan's mouth.

'I was speaking from a personal point of view.'

'Well, I . . .' Alexa gestured vaguely with one slender hand and looked away. 'I'm afraid I don't know him very well at all.'

A burst of jovial laughter drifted across the pool towards them, but Megan was only vaguely aware of her surroundings and the people milling about them. She was studying Alexa's averted face intently, and she knew somehow that her friend was not telling her the truth.

'You know something, but you don't want to tell me,' she voiced her convictions quietly, and Alexa sagged in her chair with a faint but audible sigh of resignation on her lips.

'Your powers of perception are still as sharp as ever, Megan,' she remarked, her smile tinged with guilt, but her expression sobered the next instant, and a look of distaste flashed across her beautiful face. 'News about Chad McAdam has reached me through a myriad grapevines, and I have as little faith in gossip as I have in certain newspaper reports. They can become twisted and distorted along their way to whatever medium they intend to reach.'

Nervous anxiety gripped Megan's insides and ignited a spark of doubt as to the wisdom of what she had instigated. 'Is it as bad as that?' she asked hesitantly. 'What you've heard about Chad, I mean?'

'That depends on what you want to believe.'

Those words had an ominous ring to them, and an unfamiliar tightness settled in Megan's chest. It was as if a giant hand was gripping her lungs, making it difficult for her to breathe, and she was suddenly afraid of what she was going to hear when she realised that she had finally broken through that barrier of resistance which Alexa had erected the moment Chad's name had been mentioned.

'Chad has been labelled something of a womaniser in certain circles,' Alexa began, crossing one shapely leg over the other and frowning down at her hands which she had laced together in her lap. 'His good looks and his wealth have women falling all over themselves to get his attention. He can have his pick, but he's reputed to have nothing but contempt for the women who were foolish enough to fall in love with him, and there are whispers that some of them became suicidal after they were rejected.'

Megan could not analyse her feelings at that moment, but from within the turmoil inside her there emerged a feeling of relief. Alexa had not told her very much more than she already knew, and it set her mind, if not her heart, at rest.

'Megan...' there was a hint of anxiety in the way Alexa's fingers gripped Megan's arm, 'what I've told you stems mostly from local gossip, and gossip is very often made up of ten per cent fact and ninety per cent fiction, but I do happen to be concerned for you. Chad's a handsome devil, and I can see why women might fall for him, but please...be careful.'

Be careful! A ghost of a smile touched Megan's mouth, and her clenched jaw relaxed a fraction. What Alexa was actually saying was, 'Keep an open mind, but don't fall in love with him!' It made painful sense, and quite suddenly Megan had to fight a desire to weep.

CHAPTER FIVE

MEGAN'S parents had been in no hurry to return to Louisville, and they had stayed on after the fashion show to have dinner with Megan that evening. A dark cloud bank had gathered over the Soutpansberg mountains in the distance, and it had seemed to hover there for most of that day. By nightfall it had shifted considerably closer, and the air was heavy with the promise of rain when Megan carried a tray of coffee into her lounge.

'You did well today, Megan,' Dr Peter O'Brien remarked when Megan passed him his cup of coffee. 'Your mother and I are proud of you.'

'Thanks, Dad.' Megan smiled at the lean, fair-haired man who was seated with his long legs stretched out in front of him for comfort. 'I may have neglected to say this in the past, but I have you and Mother to thank for what I've achieved, and I know I couldn't have done it without your constant support and encouragement.'

'Nonsense!' her mother contradicted her firmly. 'Your father and I have merely encouraged you to have confidence in yourself, but you've always had enough talent, ingenuity and determination to achieve your ambitions.'

Megan studied her parents thoughtfully, and smiled. 'I guess I've come a long way since those early days when I was so unsure of myself and my work as an artist.'

A knock on the bungalow door interrupted their conversation some minutes later, and Megan put down her cup to get up and answer it. She was not sure whom she had expected, but it had most certainly not been Chad, and she stood frozen, her heart hammering uncomfortably against her ribs as she stared up into those steel-grey eyes which were beginning to observe her quizzically as the seconds ticked by.

'I'm sorry I missed the fashion show this afternoon,' he said, his sensuous mouth curving in a faintly apologetic smile, 'but I believe I have to congratulate you on your success.'

'Thank you.' She emerged with difficulty from her state of frozen immobility and decided nervously that Chad looked as ominous as the weather in his black trousers and sweater. 'Won't you come in?' she invited, opening the door wider.

'I was beginning to think you wouldn't ask.' His mocking glance shifted beyond her to the two people seated in the lounge and, not in the least disturbed by their presence, he crossed the room to bow gallantly over Vivien's hand. 'It's good to see you again, Mrs O'Brien.'

Megan closed the door and moved to her father's side as he rose from his chair. 'Dad, have you met Dr McAdam?'

'Yes, we've met.' Peter O'Brien smiled pleasantly as he shook hands with Chad. 'I was hoping we would meet each other again in pleasanter circumstances.'

Megan's surprised expression did not go unnoticed, and it was Chad who explained. 'Your father and I met each other a couple of days ago when an Afrikaner bull ran amok on the common at the showgrounds, injuring itself and its handlers.'

The two men lapsed into a friendly discussion, but it unnerved Megan to witness this easy relationship which seemed to exist between them. She felt threatened for some obscure reason, but she did not have time to wonder about it. Her mother was observing her with a peculiar look in her dark eyes and, realising that she was forgetting her manners, Megan gestured Chad into a chair.

'Would you like a cup of coffee?' she offered politely, and he cast a brief, smiling glance in her direction.

'A cup of coffee would be most welcome, thank you.'

Megan escaped into the kitchen to pour an extra cup of filter coffee, but there was no escape from the sound of Chad's deep, well-modulated voice while he chatted to her parents. Everything seemed so perfectly normal, and yet it was not. If it had been Jack Harriman sitting there in her lounge with her father and her mother she would not have found it so unsettling, but it was Chad, and Megan prayed silently that her parents would not jump to the wrong conclusion about the relationship between Chad McAdam and herself.

'What made you choose to come to a place like Izilwane?' Vivien O'Brien was questioning Chad when Megan returned to the lounge, and Megan was equally curious to know the answer to that query as she handed him his cup of coffee and returned to the chair she had vacated on his arrival.

'It's always been my greatest ambition to work in a game park,' Chad explained smoothly. 'Unfortunately the opportunity never arose until a few months ago when I noticed Byron's advertisement in a veterinary journal.'

Was his ambition to work in a game park the only reason why he had applied for this post? Megan wondered with unaccustomed cynicism, observing him unobtrusively while he drank his coffee. Did the rapidly growing list of broken hearts in the city not perhaps have a far greater influence on his decision?

'Aren't you going to find it extremely difficult having to divide your time between your various business interests in Johannesburg and your work here in the game park?' Vivien persisted with her queries, but Chad appeared not to mind.

'I enjoy the challenge of both my worlds, but I'm fortunate to have extremely capable men at the helm of the various companies, and they always keep me fully informed.' He gestured expressively with one strong, sun-browned hand, and smiled faintly. 'My presence is required at board meetings and for periodic consultations, but other than that, the telephone is an efficient form of communication.'

'I happen to know that you lead a very active working life. Does that leave you with much time to socialise?'

'I'm not a social recluse, Mrs O'Brien,' Chad assured her with an amused look on his handsome, often cynical features. 'I work hard and play hard.'

'Yes, I believe you do,' Vivien murmured with a wry but equally amused smile.

Megan could hear her father talking to Chad, but she was not listening to what was actually being said between them. She had noticed that her mother was studying Chad with a strange look in her dark eyes, and she was wondering nervously at the thoughts which might be drifting through that alert and intelligent mind when an ominous rumble of thunder brought her mother's glance on a collision course with her own.

'I'll help you wash up, Megan,' she said, rising gracefully to her feet to collect the empty cups. 'It's been a most enjoyable day, but we'd better leave for home before that storm hits us.'

Megan did not argue and, taking the tray from her mother, she led the way into the kitchen, leaving Chad in the lounge with her father to continue their conversation. She worked quickly, washing the cups and saucers, and stacking them on the rack for her mother to dry with the kitchen towel she had taken off the hook against the white-tiled wall beside the sink.

'How often do you see Chad?' her mother shot the question at her, but Megan had been prepared for it.

'I see him quite often,' she confessed with a forced calmness, 'but he isn't a regular visitor, and I know he would have left long ago if you and Dad hadn't been here.'

'I'm relieved to hear that,' her mother sighed, and Megan's nervousness diminished as swiftly as the water which she was draining out of the sink.

'Don't you trust me?' she laughed softly, drying her hands on a spare kitchen towel, and turning to face her mother.

'Of course I trust you!' Vivien brushed aside Megan's query with an agitated wave of her hand. 'I'm afraid I can't say the same about Chad McAdam.'

I happen to be concerned for you. Please be careful.

Alexa's warning leapt unbidden into Megan's mind, and there was an odd tightness in her throat as she asked cautiously, 'What makes you think he can't be trusted?'

'He's too smooth, too good-looking, and...' Vivien frowned, oddly at a loss for words, then she shrugged helplessly. 'Oh, I don't know!'

'Mother...' Megan gestured reassuringly with her hands, 'I can take care of myself.'

'I know you can, my darling, but that doesn't stop me worrying about you, and I think I'd want to commit murder if anyone dared to hurt you,' Vivien declared with a vehemence which Megan had never heard before.

'Oh, Mom!' Megan's voice was choked, and she was hovering somewhere between laughter and tears when she flung her arms about her mother and hugged her tightly. 'I think you're the best mother in the world, and I love you!'

'I love you too, my pet.' Vivien smiled at her with a tender warmth in her dark eyes when they drew apart. 'That's why I shall always be concerned for you.'

A crack of thunder overhead sent them hurrying back to the lounge, and a few minutes later Megan was standing on her *stoep* with Chad, watching her parents walk at a brisk pace through the darkness to where they had parked their car beneath a mopani tree. She waved as they drove past her bungalow on their way out of the camp, but her heart was thudding nervously against her ribs as she watched the tail lights of her father's powerful Mercedes disappear around the bend in the road.

It was a dark night, and there was a tangy moisture in the hot air that whipped up against her with a force savage enough to make her rock on her feet. It moulded her white, silky dress to her slender body, accentuating her small, firm breasts, narrow waist and shapely thighs, but she had been unaware of this until she turned to find Chad observing her with more than just a casual interest in his pale eyes. She went indoors, her pulses leaping nervously as Chad followed her, and she could not quell a stab of anxiety when he closed the door to shut out the wind and the lightning which sliced across the inky sky.

'I must admit,' he began when the loud rumble of thunder had shifted off into the distance, 'I've met quite a few interesting and intelligent women since my arrival here at Izilwane, and your mother is one of them. It's incredible.'

'What's so incredible about it?' asked Megan as she moved about the lounge and made a pretence of rearranging her ornaments in a physical attempt to ease that terrible tension inside her.

'I have a strange feeling that I'm meeting an entirely new breed of women up here in the northern Transvaal. Do you think that's possible?' he asked in a voice edged with mockery.

Megan stared down at the ornament in her hands, which had been a gift from her cousin on her thirteenth birthday. It was a porcelain panther, sleek and black and dangerous as it stalked its prey, and she knew somehow that, after tonight, it would always remind her of Chad.

'It's possible that you've simply overlooked the interesting and intelligent women in favour of the kind of women who arouse your contempt,' she said, returning the ornament to its place on top of the bookshelf when the first heavy drops of wind-driven rain battered the windows.

'You make me sound like a masochist!'

'Perhaps you are... in a way.' She turned to look at him then, her glance lingering on the straight, high-bridged nose with the pinched nostrils, and the strong, jutting jaw beneath that firmly chiselled, sensuous mouth. His compelling glance drew hers, and the icy cynicism in the steel-grey depths of his eyes made her turn from him abruptly. 'I'll make us another cup of coffee.'

Chad made no attempt to prevent her leaving, and she escaped into the kitchen with a measure of relief to switch on the kettle. Her heart was beating much too hard and fast for comfort, and she was glad she could have these few moments alone to regain the composure which she had lost earlier that evening when she had found Chad standing on her doorstep.

Lightning forked across the night sky, illuminating the earth in an eerie, electrifying way, and Megan drew the curtains across the kitchen window, but nothing could shut out the terrible crack of thunder that made the floor shudder beneath her feet. The driving rain against the window was almost deafening, but she was only vaguely aware of it while she spooned instant coffee into the cups.

She was thinking about Chad, and she had to credit him with honesty. He was a man of many confusing complexities who had made no secret of his hedonistic attitude towards women, and Megan knew she had to curb her wayward feelings if she did not want to add her name to his long list of conquests.

'Your mother left her scarf behind.' Chad pulled a green silk scarf through his fingers and draped it across the arm of his chair as they sat drinking their coffee. 'Vivien O'Brien is a very clever woman, and it wouldn't surprise me if she left the scarf behind to have a valid excuse for returning later this evening.' His mouth quirked with amusement. 'I don't think she trusts me alone with her daughter.'

Megan smiled, recalling the conversation she had had with her mother. 'You're quite right, she doesn't trust you.'

'And you, Megan?' he asked, observing her with a strange intensity in his eyes which threatened to unnerve her. 'Do you trust me?'

'Give me one good reason why I should,' she responded with her own gentle brand of mockery and, to her dismay, his face tautened in anger.

'I'm not a sex maniac who goes around raping defenceless women, and I've never touched a woman who hasn't made it perfectly obvious that she desired it.'

His statement was a stinging rebuke, and humiliation surged through her, setting fire to her cheeks. That was true! Chad had kissed her and touched her because, deep down, she had actually wanted him to, and he had known it. He was an extremely attractive man and, she had no doubt, an experienced lover. The women he was accustomed to associating with would presumably need very little persuasion to satisfy his, and their own, sexual needs, but Megan wanted more from a relationship with a man than a brief physical affair.

'I was taught to believe that a man would never force his attentions on me unless I offered sufficient encouragement, but that doesn't seem to apply to you, does it?' she remarked, smiling stiffly.

'I'm a very persistent man,' he explained, his narrowed gaze flicking over her. 'When I see what I want, I make sure that I get it, and I happen to want you, Megan.'

Megan felt that familiar wave of panic rising inside her, but she suppressed it forcibly. She had to make him understand, once and for all, that she was not interested in having a meaningless, purely sexual relationship with him, and she had to stay calm if she wanted to place the necessary stress on the delivery of that message.

'I can't give you what you want, Chad,' she said flatly, her candid glance not wavering from his when he leaned forward in his chair with his elbows resting on his knees.

'Can't, or won't, Megan?' he demanded with a derisive smile.

'I *can't* and I *won't*,' she clarified her statement quietly. 'I don't want the kind of relationship you envisage, and I could never do something which would be so totally against everything I've always believed in.'

Chad's harsh laugh set her nerves quivering. 'You sound like a virgin who wants to save herself for her wedding night.'

'That's precisely what I am.' The air was suddenly static as if the electrifying storm had penetrated the solid walls of her bungalow to rage between them.

'Do you expect me to believe that you're a virgin?' Her colour came and went, giving him his answer in no uncertain terms as their glances locked in a silent battle which seemed to last an eternity before Chad rose to his feet with a look of scorn on his face. 'Well, if it's marriage you're holding out for, then you're looking at the wrong man.'

'I know.' Her voice was deadly calm, almost resigned, but those two words seemed to wail repeatedly through her mind and her body until it tore savagely at her soul. *I know, I know, I know!* If it's marriage I'm holding out for, then I'm looking at the wrong man! *I know!*

Chad left moments later, slamming the door shut behind him. Megan had watched him leave through a red mist of pain which she still could not fully understand, but she was jolted agonisingly to her senses when the handle snapped off the cup she had been holding so tightly between her hands. She stared down at it rather stupidly, then had to fight against an inexplicable desire to burst into tears.

Alexa and Revil Bradstone flew back to Johannesburg on the Monday morning with the models from Alexa's agency. It had rained all night before their departure, and for more than a week afterwards the weather at Izilwane settled into an uncomfortable pattern of hot, humid days and rainy nights.

It was during this time that Glenys Gibson arrived at Izilwane to be interviewed for the position as Chad's secretary, and two days later she moved her belongings into one of the staff bungalows. Glenys Gibson was a tall, attractive brunette who had only recently travelled north with her parents to settle in Louisville, and Megan wondered with unaccustomed cynicism whether it had been her physical appearance rather than her professional credentials which had got her the job with Chad.

It was mid-April when Megan came face to face with Chad for the first time since that night he had stormed out of her bungalow. She met him one afternoon as he was leaving Byron's office, and her heart did an odd flip-flop in her breast when those steel-grey eyes skimmed her briefly. He acknowledged her with a curt nod and walked on, and Megan stared after him, more concerned about his appearance than the fact that he had not spoken to her. He did not look well. His face had looked flushed, and he had been perspiring much too freely to blame it on the hot, humid weather.

'I have good news for you,' Byron informed Megan when she entered his office. 'The Post Office has finally laid the necessary cables to install a private line to Chad's office, and the link-up to your shop will be disconnected by tomorrow afternoon.'

Megan could not decide whether she ought to be pleased or not. It had been awkward at times, and annoying, but she could not deny that she would miss Chad's curt, often rude intrusions on her telephone conversations when he needed to make an urgent call.

'How's Frances?' she changed the subject, and Byron smiled, his rugged features softening at the mention of his wife's name.

'She's fine, considering that she's in the last stages of pregnancy, and she was wondering if you'd remembered that you promised to spend this weekend out on the farm with us.'

'That's what I came to tell you, Byron. I'm driving down to Johannesburg in the morning, so I'm afraid I'll have to put my weekend visit to Thorndale on hold.'

Megan smiled ruefully as she explained. 'A publishing company has commissioned me to do a batch of illustrative work for them, and I might be away for a week or more.'

Byron nodded with understanding, and they talked for a while longer before Megan returned to her shop, but she was in a strangely disturbed frame of mind for the rest of that day.

The rain was beating softly against her bedroom window that evening while she packed her suitcase, and she had to admit to herself that, on this particular occasion, she was actually looking forward to getting away from Izilwane for a while. The past six weeks had been tense and strained, and the long drive down to Johannesburg would give her time to think and get her life back into perspective.

She was walking towards the open suitcase on her bed with a neat pile of clothes in her arms when there was a loud hammering on her bungalow door. She dumped her clothes into the suitcase and, almost at once, the loud hammering was repeated with an unmistakable urgency.

'I'm coming!' she called out, racing across the lounge, and, flinging open the door, she found one of the restaurant waiters standing on her doorstep. His eyes were wide and frightened, and Megan's heart lurched with anxiety. 'What's wrong, Isaac? What's happened?'

'It's the doctor, Miss Megan,' he explained, his voice rising a pitch higher with concern and water dripping from his raincoat to collect in a puddle around his feet as he gestured a little wildly with his arms. 'I was told to take the doctor's dinner to his bungalow because he wasn't feeling well, but he's lying on his bed, and he's sick, Miss Megan. *Very* sick.'

Megan did not wait to hear more. She shrugged herself into her raincoat and, snatching up her keys to lock the door behind her, she ran the short distance through the rain to Chad's bungalow with Isaac in tow.

Chad's bungalow was in darkness except for the bedside light in the bedroom, and her breath caught in her throat at the sight that confronted her. Chad was naked except for black jogging shorts, and his magnificent frame was covered in a sheen of perspiration. The sheets were crumpled beneath his restlessly moving body, and he appeared to be unaware of her presence until she reached out to brush back the dark strands of hair which were clinging untidily to his damp forehead.

His skin was so hot it seemed to burn her fingers, and his heavy-lidded eyes were bloodshot and feverishly bright when he finally turned his head to look up at her. Recognition tautened his features and, brushing her hand aside impatiently, he tried to sit up, but he failed in his attempt, and sagged back weakly against the damp pillows.

'What the hell are you doing here?' he demanded, his voice slurred but angry. 'I asked Isaac to call a doctor, not you!'

Megan shrank inwardly, hurt by the knowledge that her presence was unwanted, but circumstances dictated that she should ignore his outburst.

'Chad...' she began, her voice too choked with anxiety to raise it above a whisper. 'This isn't an ordinary fever, and I'm going to make arrangements for you to be admitted to hospital.'

'No! No hospital!' he growled, rejecting her suggestion and becoming increasingly agitated. 'It's malaria. I picked up the bug on a trip to Maputo last year. I thought I'd shaken it off, but I was mistaken.'

Malaria! The word slammed an icy fear into her heart that chilled the blood in her veins.

'I'll get a doctor,' she stated resolutely, turning to the black man who was standing silent and seemingly petrified at the foot of the bed. 'Stay with him, Isaac, and I'll be back as quick as I can.'

She switched on the reading lamp in the lounge before she left and, taking a short cut across the lawn in the darkness, she dashed towards the well-lit entrance of the main building. Her breath was rasping in her throat and her heart was thudding against her ribs when she reached the telephone in the foyer. She snatched up the receiver with a hand that shook, and the switchboard responded almost immediately, giving her the outside line she requested. She punched out her home number in Louisville and waited, shivering as the water dripped from her hair into her neck and trickled down her back.

'Hurry! Oh, please hurry!' Megan whispered agitatedly, and seconds later she heard her mother's calm, familiar voice.

'Vivien O'Brien speaking.'

'Hello, Mother. Is Dad at home?' Megan demanded without wasting time on platitudes.

'He walked in a few minutes ago. Is something the matter?'

'It's Chad,' Megan explained hurriedly, not caring at that moment how her mother might interpret that note of breathless anxiety in her voice. 'He's burning up with the fever. It's a recurring bout of malaria, but he refuses to be taken to the hospital, and he needs a doctor badly.'

Vivien O'Brien had been a doctor's wife long enough to grasp the urgency of the situation, and she ended their conversation with an abrupt, 'Your father's on his way.'

Megan felt choked with emotion when she arrived back at Chad's bungalow and left her dripping raincoat draped over a chair on his *stoep*. Tears had mingled with the raindrops on her face, but she was unaware of this as she combed her fingers through her damp hair and went inside.

'Thank you, Isaac, you may go now,' she dismissed the waiter when she entered Chad's bedroom. 'I'll stay with him now.'

Isaac nodded without speaking and, casting a last, sympathetic glance at the man thrashing about feverishly on the bed, he turned and left quietly.

Megan approached the bed with more caution than before, but Chad seemed to be hovering somewhere between consciousness and oblivion as she touched his forehead and flushed cheeks tentatively with the back of her fingers. He was burning up with the fever, as she had explained to her mother, and the need to do something while she waited for her father to arrive sent her in search of a basin of cold water and a small towel.

'Megan...' Chad's voice was halting and slurred, but his thrashing body had stilled beneath her hands while she sponged him down with a cool, damp towel. 'Why are you doing this... for me?'

'Given time, you may discover that this is the way we are here in the bushveld,' she answered him evasively but truthfully. 'We never turn our back on someone who needs help.'

'Even if it's... someone you hate?'

Her hand stilled its action across his taut, flat stomach where his dark chest hair trailed into the elastic band of his shorts, and her fingers curled spasmodically into the damp towel.

'I don't hate you, Chad,' she contradicted him, her heart beating painfully against her ribs as she forced herself to sustain his feverish glance.

'You just don't... approve of the way I... choose to live, is that it?' he persisted with a suggestion of mockery in the tired smile that curved his mouth.

'You're talking too much when you should try to get some rest,' she rebuked him gently, disposing of the towel and straightening the sheet beneath him before she drew the top sheet up to his waist.

She slipped an arm beneath Chad's shoulders, and his dark head fell sideways to rest heavily against her breast when she lifted him slightly to flip the pillow on to its dry side. She lowered him on to it, and her arm was still beneath his shoulders when he raised his face to hers to capture her glance with his bloodshot eyes. His hot breath mingled with hers, and an odd weakness assailed her. It filtered into her limbs and clouded her mind to everything except the desire to lower her mouth on to his, and the feeling was so intense that she actually dipped her head a fraction before she came to her senses.

'My father is on his way, and he ought to be here any moment now,' she said, her voice stilted and a pitch higher than usual as she slipped her arm out beneath him and stood up.

'Coward.'

Megan's heart was drumming so loudly in her ears when she stooped to pick up the basin of water that it took a moment for her mind to register Chad's mocking accusation. She decided to ignore it, to pretend she had not heard, but her flaming cheeks bore witness to her embarrassment, and she left his room hurriedly before she could be subjected to yet another mocking rejoinder.

Coward? No, she was not a coward, Megan remonstrated with herself while she rinsed out the basin in Chad's kitchen and wrung out the towel. There was no sense, however, in playing with fire when she knew she would burn her fingers. Was there?

Chad was lying with his eyes closed when she returned to his room a few minutes later, and she pulled up a chair quietly to seat herself beside his bed. He was restless, moving his head from side to side on the pillow while he muttered unintelligibly, and she sighed despairingly when she saw his tanned skin glistening with a layer of fresh perspiration.

The fever was sapping his vitality before her very eyes and leaving him drained while she sat there watching and waiting. She was listening to the rain pelting the windows and dripping down the gutters, but she was praying silently that her father would arrive soon. She might not approve of Chad's life-style, and she might be repelled by his distorted opinion of women, but she could not bear to see him so completely at the mercy of something which he could not control. Her compassionate heart bled for him, but it was something infinitely stronger than pity which was rising from the depths of her soul in a quest for recognition, and Megan had neither the strength nor the will to suppress it at that moment.

A tired sigh escaped her, and she passed a shaky hand over her eyes as she sagged back into the armchair. It was senseless trying to deny those feelings which had been pounding inside her these past weeks. She had labelled them with everything except the truth, but she had to face up to it now.

She was in love with Chad. It was a hopeless love without a future, but trying to curb it had been as futile as trying to curb the rampant flow of a river in flood.

Megan groaned inwardly. Why did it have to be this way? Why did she have to fall in love with a man like Chad McAdam who would never have anything to offer her in return?

Her vision blurred with angry, despairing tears, but she dashed them away with the back of her hand, and rose from the armchair with a thankful sigh on her lips when the lights of an approaching vehicle flashed across the window before it came to a crunching halt at the entrance to the bungalow.

CHAPTER SIX

MEGAN left Chad's bedside and crossed the lounge with its sturdy pine furniture and colourful rugs. She opened the door and, staring out into the darkness, saw her father's tall, lean figure sprinting through the rain from his parked car on to the thatch-covered *stoep* where she stood in the doorway, silhouetted against the inside lights.

'I'm sorry I took a bit long to get here, Megan, but I was in the shower when you called,' her father explained briskly, shedding his wet raincoat before he entered the bungalow.

Megan nodded without speaking, her throat too choked to utter a sound, and turned quickly to lead the way through the lounge into the bedroom.

Chad was moving about restlessly on the bed when they entered the room. His body glistened with perspiration, but he appeared to be shivering, and Megan felt the burning dampness of his skin against her palm when she placed a calming hand on his shoulder. 'My father is here, Chad.'

He turned his head on the pillow in response to her voice and, lifting his heavy eyelids, focused his feverish eyes first on Megan and then on her father. 'Goodness knows I'm sorry you had to be called out in this filthy weather, Dr O'Brien, but I feel lousy,' he muttered hoarsely.

'If it's malaria, as you say, then I don't doubt you feel lousy.' Peter O'Brien's smile was sympathetic when he put his medical bag on the armchair beside the bed and opened it. 'Let's take a look at you and make sure.'

Megan moved out of the way and watched in silence while her father examined Chad, and she had never admired him more for his calm professionalism than at

93

that moment. It inspired her confidence, but it did not ease her anxiety in this instance. Chad was slipping into a state of semi-consciousness, and it frightened her.

'I'm going to give him a double dose of darachlor to start off with,' her father enlightened her when he had finally completed his examination. 'And I'm sure Chad won't need to be told that he'll have to take a daily course of these tablets for the next six weeks.'

'Yes, I know, and . . . it's a . . . confounded nuisance,' Chad responded unexpectedly to Peter O'Brien's statement, and his slurred, halting voice was tinged with irritation.

'I imagine it is a nuisance,' Peter agreed, producing a phial of tablets from his bag, 'but it's the only way you're going to rid yourself of this malaria bug.'

Megan poured water into a glass from the carafe on the bedside cupboard, but it was her father who helped Chad take the tablets, and, after lowering him on to the pillows and making him comfortable, he gestured that Megan should follow him out of the room.

'He shouldn't be left alone, Megan,' he said, seating himself at the small writing desk in the lounge and producing a prescription pad and pen from his bag. 'I'll arrange with the hospital to send someone out to special him through the night.'

Megan shook her head. 'That won't be necessary.'

Her trip to Johannesburg would simply have to wait. She would have a message sent to the publishing company first thing in the morning, and if this delay resulted in the loss of the commission they had offered her, then so be it. She was not going to leave now while Chad was so ill.

'The fever will have to take its course, Megan,' her father warned, 'and there'll be chills and possible delirium.'

'I'll manage,' she insisted, squaring her slim shoulders and holding her father's troubled glance with a resolute expression on her face.

'Very well,' her father sighed resignedly, lowering his gaze to write out a prescription before he reached into his medical bag for a phial of tablets. 'I'm leaving Chad with a few darachlor tablets which should last until he can have this prescription filled,' he explained and, delving into his bag, he produced yet another phial of tablets. 'There's no way of knowing how long it will take for the fever to break. It could be anything from one to three days, but it should help if you give him two of these tablets at four-hourly intervals.'

Megan's face was suddenly pale and pinched as she picked up the phials and studied the labels. She now had a clearer vision of what lay in store for her, and she dared not make an error with the medication her father had prescribed for Chad.

'I'll call in again first thing in the morning,' her father promised gravely, snapping his medical bag shut and rising to his feet to tower over her. 'If you should need me during the night you only have to call. You know that, don't you?'

'Yes, I know,' Megan murmured gratefully. 'Thank you, Dad.'

She raised her glance to find her father observing her with a look of deep concern in his blue eyes, and she tried to conjure up a reassuring smile, but failed. The tears were much too close for comfort, and she looked away again, fighting a desperate, silent battle for control.

'I'm sure you've given a thought to the fact that your actions might be misinterpreted by the family.'

Megan nodded in reply, her throat too tight to speak. She had considered the implication of her actions, but she had chosen not to dwell on it. There would be time enough later for her to face the consequences and to find a way to deal with them.

'Don't worry, Megan.' Her father put an arm about her shoulders and gave her a comforting hug. 'Chad's going to be all right.'

A few moments later Megan was watching the tail lights of her father's Mercedes disappearing into the dark, rainy night. Hot tears stung her eyelids, but she blinked them away as she went inside and closed the door behind her to shut out the cool, damp air.

She remained at Chad's bedside through that night and on through the long, stifling hours of the following day, but her father and Byron gave her all the moral support she needed. The restaurant staff constantly plied her with food, but she could not recall eating any of it while she nursed Chad tirelessly throughout those long hours while his body was racked alternately with fever and chills.

The day stretched into night again, and it was some time after midnight, when Megan had dozed off in the high-backed armchair beside the bed, that Chad lapsed into a bout of delirium, and the sound of his throaty voice, raised in anger, made her sit up with a guilty start. She had never encountered anything like this before, but her natural instinct was to comfort him, and, when he flung out an arm in her direction, she rose at once to take his hand between her own.

'Chad, what is it? What's wrong?' she demanded anxiously, but he did not hear her.

He was breathing unevenly, and the expressions flitting across his unshaven, sweat-drenched features alternated between extreme anxiety and anger as he tossed about in an agitated frenzy. At times he gripped Megan's hand so tightly that she had to bite down hard on her lip not to cry out with the agony of it while he rambled on incessantly, the pitch of his voice rising and falling according to the level of his distress. Much of what he said made no sense to her, but a few disjointed sentences filtered through which she found enlightening.

'They said you'd never come back ... Should have believed them ... Never trust a woman ... You're right, Father ... Women are all the same ... Bed them, don't

wed them... Shouldn't have gone away, Mother...
Trusted you... Let me down.'

Megan swallowed hard and fought back the tears, her
fingers tightening about Chad's when she felt the
anguished tremors flowing from his body into her own.
He had given her an unexpected glimpse of the past, and
she suffered his torment as if it were her own.

'Megan...' Chad's feverish eyes searched her face, but
she could not be sure that he actually saw her. 'Can
I...trust you?'

She felt too choked to speak, but she cleared her throat
and made the attempt. 'You can trust me, Chad.'

'No! You're lying!' he accused harshly, the dim
bedside light accentuating the angles and planes of a face
which had become distorted with a savage anger, and he
flung her hand aside as if he could not bear her touch.
'Lies...all lies...can't trust a woman.'

'Oh, Chad!' His name spilled from her lips on a sigh
of despair, and she turned from him, her eyes brimming
with tears.

'Don't go away again...don't go away...need you...'

Megan could not be sure whether Chad was speaking
to her, or referring to his mother, but his wildly thrashing
movements made her turn back hastily and, blinking at
the stinging moisture in her eyes, she slipped her hand
into his once again and gripped it firmly.

'I'm not going away,' she assured him with a calmness
which belied the emotional storm raging inside her. 'Trust
me. I'll stay for as long as you need me, and that's a
promise.'

Chad subjected her to a long, hard stare, clearly
doubting her, but it was, perhaps, the sincerity in her
voice which finally filtered through to his subconscious
mind. He relaxed visibly against the pillows and, sighing
deeply, closed his eyes and slipped once again into that
fretful world of oblivion.

· Megan tried to swallow down that aching lump in her
throat, but she failed, and neither could she control her

tears. They spilled from her lashes and rolled freely down her cheeks while she assimilated the facts. Drawing from his own experiences during his childhood, and influenced, perhaps, by his disillusioned, embittered father, Chad's need for someone he could love and trust had been buried deep over the years for fear of being hurt.

He had revealed something to Megan in his state of delirium which he would not willingly have revealed to anyone else, and she must never let him guess that he had bared his soul to her in this way. She had been an intruder on his private thoughts and feelings, but it had, at least, afforded her that glimmer of understanding which she had sought for so long.

She loved him...oh, how she loved him...but he must never suspect. Never! His conscious mind had no need of her love, and she could not bear the thought of being held up for ridicule.

Megan's tears finally dried on her cheeks and, freeing her hand from Chad's, she left the room to fill the basin with fresh, tepid water to sponge him down.

The remainder of that night passed slowly and uneventfully and, as dawn approached, Chad became considerably calmer. He appeared to be sleeping naturally for the first time, and Megan leaned back in the armchair, closing her tired eyes, but she did not sleep. Her mind remained alert to the slightest sound, and it was about six-thirty that morning when she heard the front door open.

Byron entered the room moments later. He drew aside the curtains at the window to admit the early morning light and, casting a brief, searching glance at Megan's hollow-eyed face, he approached the bed to brush the back of his fingers across Chad's forehead and lean, unshaven cheeks.

'The crisis is over,' he said, smiling at Megan across Chad's inert figure on the bed.

The crisis might be over for Chad, but it had only just begun for Megan. She would have to learn to cope with her feelings, and she was not so sure that she was going to succeed.

'I'll stay with him for a while,' offered Byron, and his glance was critical as it flicked over Megan. 'I suggest you go to your bungalow and get into bed before you drop with fatigue.'

'Oh, no, I can't! I can't leave——'

'What Chad needs now is rest,' he interrupted her with a gleam of teasing mockery in his eyes, 'and he can do that without someone having to hold his hand.'

Megan realised with an embarrassing start that she was still holding Chad's warm, rough hand in her own, and she released it with a self-conscious smile.

'I guess you're right,' she agreed, blushing profusely as she rose to her feet and switched off the bedside light.

Chad's features looked calm and relaxed. The fever had left him and the crisis was over, as Byron had said. There was nothing more she could do for him, and she was suddenly so dreadfully tired that she wondered if she still had enough strength left to walk the short distance from Chad's bungalow to her own.

'I have a message for you.' Megan paused in the doorway, and had to clutch at the frame to steady herself as she turned slowly to face Byron. 'A Mr John Driscoll from the publishing company called yesterday afternoon,' he informed her. 'They want you to be in Johannesburg by tomorrow afternoon at the latest.'

Megan nodded mutely and left, the brightness of the early morning sunlight blinding her momentarily when she stepped outside, and it seemed a tremendous effort to put one foot in front of the other as she walked the short distance to her bungalow.

The knowledge that John Driscoll considered her work good enough to warrant a postponement of their meeting should have elated her, but, oddly enough, she felt nothing at all. It was this lack of feeling that made her realise, for the first time, how exhausted she actually was.

She had difficulty unlocking the door to her bungalow, and there was a strange buzzing noise in her head when she finally entered her bedroom and closed the door behind her.

Everything was still exactly as she had left it two nights ago. Was it only two nights ago that Isaac had hammered on her door to tell her that Chad was ill? Or was it an eternity ago? Megan could not quite remember as she dragged the open suitcase off the bed so that it landed with a thud on the floor. Her bed looked incredibly inviting and, too tired to change out of her clothes, she flung herself on to it and promptly went to sleep.

Megan showered and washed her hair before getting dressed for dinner. This was her last night in the hotel and, after ten hectic and seemingly endless days in Johannesburg, she was more than ready to return to the peace and tranquillity of her home in Louisville.

She was trying to decide what to wear when the shrill ring of the telephone interrupted her. John Driscoll had said he might give her a call before she left, and, tightening the belt of her towelling robe about her waist, she seated herself on the edge of the bed and lifted the receiver to her ear.

'Megan O'Brien speaking.'

'Hello, Megan.'

The voice was deep and masculine, but it was not the voice she had expected to hear, and her heart hammered a little wildly against her ribs.

'This is an unexpected surprise, Chad,' she said, injecting a cool politeness into her voice.

'I'm in Johannesburg on business for a couple of days, and Dorothy told me which hotel you'd be staying at,' he answered her unspoken query. 'Are you perhaps free this evening to have dinner with me?'

Megan fingered the belt of her robe nervously and glanced at the suitcase which lay open on her bed. 'I ... think so ... yes.'

'You don't sound very sure.'

'I'm leaving tomorrow, and I still have some packing to do,' she explained, 'but I'd like to have dinner with you.'

'Good! I'll be there at seven to pick you up.'

'I'll meet you in the foyer,' she agreed before Chad ended their conversation abruptly.

She replaced the receiver and combed her fingers nervously through her short, damp curls. She was not sure that it had been wise of her to agree so readily to have dinner with Chad. She had not seen him before her departure from Izilwane. She had slept like someone drugged after those long hours of nursing him and, too wary to risk making a trip to Chad's bungalow, she had relied on Byron's information that he was recovering rapidly from his bout of malaria.

She drew a shaky breath and glanced at her wrist watch where it lay on the bedside cupboard beside the telephone. Chad would be arriving at the hotel within less than an hour, and, leaping to her feet, she galvanised herself into action, drying her hair, deciding what she ought to wear, and taking particular care with her make-up. Nervous excitement had quickened the pace of her heart when she finally stood back to survey herself in the full-length mirror.

'Not bad,' she complimented herself. She looked calm and composed despite that well of anxiety at the pit of her stomach, and the rich burgundy of her long-sleeved evening dress added a glowing warmth to her features. The fine woollen material clung softly to the gentle curve of her breasts and hips, accentuating her femininity, but Megan was no longer considering her appearance when she walked across the room towards the built-in cupboard with the slatted doors. The night air could be chilly in Johannesburg at that time of the year, and she draped her suede coat about her shoulders before she left her room to take the lift down to the foyer.

Chad was rising from an armchair beside a potted plant in the spacious foyer when she stepped out of the lift, and her heart skipped a suffocating beat at the sight of him. His brown leather jacket emphasised the width of his shoulders while the brown slacks and beige polo-necked sweater heightened his tanned complexion, and Megan's legs felt as if they were rapidly turning to jelly beneath her as she walked towards him across the thickly carpeted foyer.

'Am I late?' she asked, searching his rigid face for signs of his recent illness, but finding none.

'I was a few minutes early.'

His stern features did not relax, and Megan felt that well of anxiety spread inside her as she accompanied him out of the hotel to where he had parked his blue Porsche.

She was already having grave doubts about her decision to have dinner with him when he slid into the driver's seat beside her and turned the key in the ignition. She stole a quick glance at him, but his chiselled profile did not encourage conversation as he edged his car into the traffic, and she realised with a sinking heart that it was too late now to change her mind.

'Where are we going?' she felt compelled to ask some minutes later when Chad turned off on to a road which led away from the city centre.

'I've arranged for us to have dinner at my home.' He stared straight ahead of him at the traffic, but in the dashboard light Megan could see his mouth curving in a faintly mocking smile. 'Do you have any objections?'

The frightened beat of her heart subsided slowly as her rational mind took charge of the situation. Chad was obviously going to do his best to unnerve her, and she was not going to allow him that victory.

'Would you change our dinner venue if I objected?'

'No.'

His abrupt answer made her smile wryly into the dark interior of the car. 'I didn't think you would.'

Chad did not respond to that unaccustomed hint of sarcasm in her voice, and they drove on in silence towards the outskirts of Johannesburg.

The atmosphere between them was incredibly tense and strained, and Megan was beginning to think they would never reach their destination when Chad steered the Porsche on to a single-lane road leading off to the left. They passed beneath a stone arch at the entrance to a long, curving, tree-lined avenue, and Megan caught a glimpse of lights up ahead. She was not sure what she had expected to see, but she was totally unprepared for what she finally encountered when they emerged from the avenue of tall poplar trees.

Chad's home was a sprawling Cape Dutch style house. With no sign of another house in the vicinity, she imagined that his home had to be set on several acres of land, and she regretted the fact that the darkness obscured so much from her view.

'My father bought this piece of land and had this house built when he married my mother,' Chad explained when they got out of the car, and his hand was firm beneath her elbow when they walked up the shallow steps towards the gabled entrance.

Megan glanced up at the ornamentation above the heavy oak door, and found it ironic to see Cupid, his bow and arrow poised, carved into the wood above the entrance to a house in which love had gone so dreadfully awry.

The door was opened as if on cue by a white-coated black man, and Chad's hand shifted from Megan's elbow to the hollow of her back as he ushered her into the spacious entrance hall where the heavy crystal chandelier hanging from the ceiling shed prisms of light across the earthy-coloured tiles on the floor.

'You're back sooner than I expected, sir.'

'Harry, this is Miss O'Brien,' Chad introduced Megan, 'and if I'm back sooner than you expected, then it's because Miss O'Brien happens to be a very punctual lady.'

Harry inclined his head at Megan in a silent but polite greeting before he relieved her of her coat and draped it carefully on the old-fashioned stand in the hall.

'Will you have something to drink before dinner, Megan?' offered Chad as he took her through to the living-room where their footsteps were muted by the thick pile of the carpet on the floor. 'A glass of wine, perhaps?'

'A glass of wine would be lovely, thank you,' she agreed with a nervous smile, and glanced about her with interest while Chad walked away from her towards the heavy oak cabinet in the corner of the room.

The living-room was furnished with antiques and, despite Megan's ignorance on the subject, some of the pieces were undoubtedly priceless. The plush seats and backrests of the ornately carved rosewood bench and chairs had been covered with a cool blue velvet that matched the curtains drawn across the high sash windows, and on a low-slung stinkwood table against an inner wall stood a tall, narrow-necked vase which was obviously of Oriental origin.

It was an exquisitely furnished room, but it lacked that warm, lived-in feeling, and that was such a pity, Megan was thinking when Chad handed her a long-stemmed glass of wine.

She slid her fingers around the delicate crystal-cut bowl to avoid touching his hand, and sipped the dry white wine in the hope of steadying that nervous flutter in her stomach.

'I presume this is where you usually entertain your lady-friends?' she questioned him caustically, and his mouth tightened with a suggestion of annoyance, making her realise her mistake even before he answered her.

'You're the first woman I've ever brought to my home.'

Megan regretted her impulsive query and, feeling awkward, she turned from him to study the large, heavily framed painting which was hanging above the stone fireplace. It was a portrait in oils, and the subject was a harsh-faced, dark-eyed man with silver streaks slicing through the coppery hair at his temples.

'That's my father.'

'I gathered as much,' Megan remarked, turning her back on that disapproving and embittered face in the portrait to seat herself in the chair Chad had indicated. 'You have your father's mouth and square jaw, but the resemblance ends there.'

'My sister Matty is almost the image of my father.' Chad set his glass on the low, ornately carved table with the glass top to take off his leather jacket. 'Perhaps that's why my father spoiled her so much,' he added, smiling cynically as he retrieved his glass and seated himself on the chair facing hers.

Megan was remembering some of the things Chad had told her about himself and his family, and most especially she was recalling what he had said during his bout of delirium. She had suspected then that there was no fondness between him and his sister, but there was no doubt in her mind about it now.

'Did you have a good relationship with your father?'

She had not intended to ask him that, but she was finding it difficult to behave naturally when she was so intensely aware of his long-limbed, muscular frame lounging in the chair close to hers. She could see him in her mind, stripped down to his jogging shorts and his body racked with fever. The scent of him and the feel of him would remain with her forever after those long hours of nursing him, but she dared not think about that now.

She leaned back in her chair and tried to relax, but her fingers trembled around the fragile stem of the glass as she raised it to her lips, and the sardonic lift of Chad's eyebrows told her that her discomfiture had not gone unnoticed.

'My father taught me a lot.'

Yes, she thought sadly. He taught you never to love and trust anyone—especially a woman—and, in the process of learning, his cynicism and bitterness became yours.

The ticking of the old-fashioned clock on the mantelshelf seemed to increase in volume during the ensuing silence, and Megan said the first thing that came to mind in an attempt to ease that build-up of nervous tension inside her.

'What made you decide finally to become a vet rather than going full-time into your father's business?'

'I was forced to sit in on many of my father's business deals. I don't regret it. I learned a lot from those sessions with my father, but it didn't appeal to me as a full-time career. I wanted an outdoor job, preferably a medical one which would involve animals, and that's why I decided to become a veterinary surgeon.' He stretched his long, muscular legs out in front of him, and smiled as he studied the tips of his suede shoes, but the smile did not reach his steel-grey eyes. 'I never considered it at the time, but, the way things are, I now have the best of both worlds.'

'That's true, I suppose,' she agreed, leaning forward to set her empty glass on the low table between them, and they lapsed once again into a silence which was threatening to become awkward when the white-coated black man appeared in the doorway.

'Shall I serve dinner, sir?'

Chad glanced at the gold watch strapped to his lean wrist and nodded. 'Thank you, Harry.'

He drained his glass and, rising, held out his hand to Megan. He drew her to her feet, his fingers warm and firm about hers, and it sent an unwanted current of awareness tripping across her nerve-ends. Chad felt it too, she could see it in his eyes and feel it in the tightening of his fingers about hers, and it left her oddly breathless when they walked out of the living-room and across the tiled entrance hall towards the dining-room.

CHAPTER SEVEN

CHAD'S home was a showpiece of grandeur, with a banqueting hall in which twenty or more dinner guests could be accommodated with ease at a long table which was an attractive mixture of stinkwood and yellowwood. Chandeliers, hanging low from the beamed ceiling, were reflected in mirrors above ornately carved antique dressers, and gilt-framed paintings, all originals by well-known artists, adorned the walls.

It was an awe-inspiring sight, but the room where Megan dined with Chad was smaller and much less ostentatious. The lights against the panelled walls had been dimmed and, against the white damask tablecloth, the silverware sparkled in the flickering light of the candles in the silver candelabrum on the table.

The setting was perfect for a relaxed and intimate dinner for two with Harry coming and going discreetly to serve the various courses of the superb meal which had been prepared for them, but Megan could not recall afterwards what she had eaten, or if she had eaten at all. She was much too aware of that wall of tension which had built up between Chad and herself. It was there beneath the surface of the platitudes they had exchanged all evening, like a strong and dangerous undercurrent, and it set her nerves on edge.

Harry served them their coffee and left, and it was then that Chad broached the subject of his recent bout of malaria. 'I was still too weak to come to you before you left Izilwane,' he said, 'but you could have come to me. Why didn't you, Megan?'

'I wanted to,' she confessed with her usual honesty as she sustained his probing glance across the candlelit table.

'What stopped you?'

'We weren't exactly on the best of terms before your bout of malaria, and afterwards...' She faltered and lowered her gaze nervously to fiddle with the teaspoon in her saucer. 'Well, I wasn't sure that I'd be welcome,' she added truthfully.

'You took it upon yourself to nurse me through thirty-six hours of fever and heaven knows what else, and you weren't sure you'd be welcome?' There was an explosive little silence, then Chad laughed harshly. 'Oh, come now, Megan, you surely don't expect me to believe that, do you?'

'You didn't want me there in the first place,' she reminded him with a forced calmness, 'and I couldn't think of any reason why you would want me there afterwards.'

'It would have given me the opportunity to thank you instead of having to wait until now to do so.'

Megan looked up into those steel-grey eyes observing her so intently, and looked away again with a measure of distaste. She did not want gratitude from Chad! She wanted...!

'You don't have to thank me,' she said coldly, reining in her thoughts and raising her cup to her lips to gulp down the last mouthful of coffee.

'It's common courtesy to thank someone for services rendered.'

That hint of laughter in his voice snapped the level of her tolerance. She could take so much, and no more!

'Is that the reason I've been treated to this rare honour of dining with you in your home this evening?' she demanded with that icy sarcasm which was so totally alien to her nature, and looked up to see the amusement draining from his pale eyes to leave them cold and disapproving.

'I assumed that you might have had your fill of the city racket after ten days in Johannesburg, and, since I'm not partial to crowded restaurants, my home seemed to be the most suitable place for a quiet dinner and a private chat.'

Megan winced inwardly. His voice had been strangely calm and devoid of anger, but every word had had the effect of a stinging rap over the knuckles, and she leaned back in her chair with a rueful smile on her lips.

'I'm sorry.'

'It was an understandable error,' he conceded gravely, and the tension seemed to ease between them when they lingered at the table over a second cup of coffee.

Megan was beginning to feel pleasantly relaxed when they finally returned to the living-room where the fire had been lit in the stone fireplace. The room had warmed up considerably, and she did not object when Chad took her hand to draw her down on to the bench beside him.

'Did I make any shocking revelations while I was *non compos mentis*?' he questioned her unexpectedly, but Megan was instantly on her guard.

'You rambled on a bit about women all being the same, and that they were not to be trusted,' she answered him cautiously, staring down at the rich cream of the carpet beneath her feet.

'That sounds familiar,' he laughed shortly. 'Did I perhaps expound on anything else worth repeating?'

'No,' she lied. 'Not that I can recall.'

She looked up then to see the smile fade from his eyes to leave in its place a strange glitter that quickened the rhythm of her pulses. The tension piled high between them once again, but this time Megan recognised it for what it was. It was a simple case of wariness. They had been circling each other mentally all evening, but the time had come for one of them to make the first move.

'Where is this leading us, Megan?'

That was ingenious. Chad was inviting her to take the first step, but, probably for the first time in his life, he was exercising caution, and she had to admire him for it.

'I don't know what you mean,' she replied, pleading ignorance to give herself more time, but Chad foiled her evasive tactics when he slid his arm along the back of the bench behind her shoulders and tipped her face up to his with his free hand.

'It can't stop here, and we both know it. From the very beginning we've sparked off something in each other which refuses to be denied, so it has to lead somewhere.'

His compelling glance held hers, his eyes challenging and probing while his thumb gently traced the curve of her lower lip. There was a trembling deep inside her, a need which she could no longer ignore, and she rose jerkily to her feet, knowing it would be senseless to go on pretending that she did not know what he was talking about.

'I don't know if I want it to lead anywhere,' she confessed when she held her hands out to the log fire crackling in the grate and felt the heat of it against her cold palms.

'I don't blame you for feeling that way, Megan.' The gravity in that smooth, velvety voice was unfamiliar on the ears, and her body tensed as she felt him come up behind her. 'I've behaved like a cad, but you've had me running round in uncomfortable circles in an attempt to reach some sort of understanding with you, and I don't happen to like it.'

Chad was standing so close to her that she could feel the heat of his body against her back. If she moved just a fraction, their bodies would touch, and there was nothing she wanted more than to feel the strength of his arms about her, but she dared not dwell on that enticing thought.

'I can't accept the moral code by which you live, and you can't accept mine.' She gestured expressively with her hands and caught her quivering lip between her teeth to steady it. 'I don't think that's a very sound basis on which to build a relationship.'

'I have to agree with you on that score, but I can't shake off the feeling that there's something between us which deserves to be explored.'

'Oh, Chad!' she sighed helplessly, his words finding an echo in her hungry heart.

'You feel it too, don't you?' His hands were warm and heavy on her shoulders as he turned her to face him. 'Don't you, Megan?'

'Yes,' she whispered resignedly. 'Yes, I do.'

His taut features relaxed visibly, making her realise how important her answer had been to him, and a melting warmth erupted inside her. He was, for that brief moment, stripped of his usual arrogance, and his uncertainty touched her as nothing had ever done before.

'If I give you my word that I shan't rush you into anything you don't want, do you think we could explore it together?'

Megan answered his question with one of her own. 'Have you considered the possibility that this could lead to something which might leave us both hurt and disillusioned?'

'That's a risk we'll have to take.' His hands tightened on her shoulders with an urgency that matched the burning intensity of his eyes. 'Are you willing to take that chance with me?'

The clock on the mantelshelf ticked away the seconds while Megan sought the answer within herself. She was allowing herself to be coaxed along a path which could only lead to pain, but she could not turn her back on it.

'Yes, Chad,' Megan heard herself answering him firmly and resolutely despite all her misgivings. 'I'm willing to take that chance with you.'

A muscle leapt in his jaw, and one hand slipped into her honey-gold hair at the base of her skull while the other shifted down her back to draw her into the hard curve of his body. His warm lips brushed against her forehead, her eyelids and her cheeks before they finally came to rest on her mouth. He teased her lips with feather-light kisses, exploring and savouring until Megan thought she would go mad with the desire for more.

Her hands clenched against his wide chest, her fingers curling into the expensive sweater to convey a silent, eager message of their own, and Chad's restraint deserted him. He ravaged her parted lips with a fierce hunger that made her senses reel, and her sanity was questionable when his hands gripped her buttocks firmly to draw her closer to his aroused body. Megan wanted him to touch her; she wanted to feel her body come alive beneath the touch of his hands, and she wanted it so badly that she trembled violently in the grip of that aching warmth surging into her loins.

'You don't know what you're doing to me!' he muttered thickly, releasing her abruptly to put on his leather jacket.

'I'm sorry,' she whispered, feeling lost and cold without his arms about her, and he rounded on her with a look of unconcealed frustration on his face.

'Don't apologise,' he said, reaching for her hand and raising it to his lips. 'It isn't your fault that I happen to want you with the impatience of an adolescent in search of his first sexual conquest,' he growled into her palm.

I want you, too, she could have said, and it was true, but she wanted more than a brief physical encounter with Chad. She wanted what he could never give her, and it was this knowledge that put such a stringent guard on her tongue.

'It's time I took you back to your hotel,' he said abruptly, releasing her hand, and when she glanced at the clock on the mantelshelf she was surprised to see that it was almost eleven o'clock.

Chad helped her into her coat in the hall, and they drove back to the hotel in comparative silence, but this time the silence was not fraught with the tension which had been there between them earlier that evening.

'What time will you be leaving in the morning?' he questioned her as they stood in the lift which was taking them up to the fourth floor of the hotel.

'I'm hoping to leave immediately after breakfast.' She glanced up at him and studied his stern profile curiously. 'How long do you think you'll be staying in Johannesburg?'

'I have a couple of meetings lined up, but I should be leaving after lunch on Friday.'

His glance captured hers, and the warm smile curving his sensuous mouth heightened the reality of what had transpired between them. He wanted her—he had said so. She could see it in his eyes even now, but he was in complete control of his emotions. And that was more than she could say for herself, Megan realised when she recalled her uninhibited response to his kisses.

'Are you going straight through to Izilwane, or will you be spending the weekend with your parents in Louisville?'

Megan wrenched her gaze from his when she heard the lift doors slide open. 'I'll be in Louisville with my parents,' she said, stepping out of the lift ahead of him, and the hard, erratic beat of her heart was threatening to suffocate her as he accompanied her down the carpeted passage to her room. 'I have a mountain of sketches to do, and my studio at home is the best place to work,' she explained.

Chad took her key from her and unlocked her bedroom door, but he made no attempt to go in. 'I'll come and see you as soon as I can,' he said, smiling faintly as he tipped up her face and kissed her lightly on the lips. 'Goodnight, and drive carefully.'

Megan watched him walk away from her with those long, lithe strides, and she was tempted to call him back, but she bit down hard on her tongue to quell the impulse as she entered her room and locked the door firmly behind her. Chad had promised not to rush her into something which she did not want, but she suspected his need was as strong as her own, and she was no longer sure that her rigid principles would survive as a safety barrier if it were put to the test.

It was a shattering thought, and it left her heated with embarrassment and something else which she was determined to ignore. 'What you need, my girl, is a cold, sobering shower,' she told herself, and, acting on her own advice, she stripped down to her skin and stepped beneath the jet of cold water in the shower cubicle.

Megan drove away from Johannesburg with an uncommon reluctance on Thursday morning. The northbound road took her past Pretoria towards Warmbaths, a town which was noted for its hot springs. *Biela Bela*, the water that boils on its own, the Twanas had called the hot springs long before it had been exploited for its therapeutic value.

She broke the long journey home to stop in Potgietersrus with its tree-lined streets and beautiful subtropical gardens. She lingered long enough to have a cup of tea and a sandwich at a roadside restaurant for travellers on the outskirts of the town, and then she drove on to Louisville, which lay beyond the Soutpansberg mountains.

The winding road on the mountain pass sliced through pine plantations and, inevitably, there were trucks transporting lumber from the various camps in the area. It made the final stretch of Megan's journey exhausting in the oppressive afternoon heat, and when she arrived in Louisville her parents' home felt like a cool oasis in a scorching desert.

She was relaxing in the living-room with her mother, sipping a long, cool drink and assimilating everything that had happened during the past twenty-four hours, when the telephone rang in the hall. Vivien got up to answer it, and put her head around the door a moment later.

'It's for you, Megan,' she said, and Megan put her glass down on the table beside her chair when she rose to take the call.

There was an odd look on Vivien's face as she brushed past Megan to return to her chair in the living-room, and Megan's smooth brow creased in a slight frown when she lifted the receiver to her ear.

'Hello? Megan O'Brien speaking.'

'I'm in the middle of a board meeting, Megan, but I wanted to make sure you'd arrived home safely.'

Megan's heart leapt at the sound of Chad's deep, velvety voice, and she leaned dizzily against the wall beside the telephone table. 'I arrived half an hour ago.'

'You must be tired.'

'I am,' she confessed, finding his concern oddly touching.

'I shan't keep you, then,' he ended their brief conversation abruptly. 'See you soon.'

Megan returned to the living-room and curled up comfortably on her chair before she picked up her glass to gulp down a mouthful of her iced drink. Her mother was working on a tapestry, the needle flashing as it disappeared into the material and reappeared in rapid succession, and Megan observed her in silence until she felt compelled to say something in order to break the oddly strained silence between them.

'That was Chad.'

'I know,' her mother replied without looking up from her tapestry, and Megan encountered a faint stab of uneasiness that made her shift uncomfortably in her chair.

'He called to make sure that I'd arrived home safely,' she heard herself explaining.

'That was thoughtful of him.' Vivien looked up from her tapestry for the first time, her dark gaze gently probing. 'I heard that he left yesterday to attend a board meeting in Johannesburg, and I gather he contacted you.'

'I had dinner with him last night,' Megan confessed, but she withheld the fact that the venue had been at Chad's home.

'I suppose that was Chad's way of showing his gratitude for the long hours you nursed him,' her mother
filed her actions neatly into an acceptable category.

'Yes, I suppose it was,' Megan agreed, deciding it
would be wiser not to say more, and she went up to her
room a few minutes later for a shower and a change of
clothing before dinner.

The conversation at the dinner table that evening was
as lively and enthusiastic as always, and Peter and Vivien
O'Brien listened attentively while Megan related everything that had happened during her stay in the city. Chad
was never mentioned, and Megan preferred to keep it
that way.

The small cottage in the grounds of her parents' home
was an ideal place to work on the illustrations she had
been commissioned to do. She had long ago trans-
formed the cottage into a studio and workshop for
herself, and she started working in earnest on Friday
morning, making preliminary sketches within the
framework of the story, which had been written for
children.

It was an exciting and absorbing task, but at odd moments she found herself thinking about Chad instead of
working. There's something between us which deserves
to be explored, he had said, and she had finally agreed
to something which her logical mind warned could only
bring her heartache, but, loving him as much as she did,
it was a chance she had to take.

But she did not want to think about Chad. She had
work to do, and she would never get it done if she allowed this intrusion on her thoughts.

Megan worked steadily throughout that day, and she
was up again before breakfast on Saturday morning. By
twelve-thirty that day she had started working on the
first small painting in oils of little children playing in a
field carpeted with white, yellow, and orange
namaqualand daisies. It was a bright, cheerful scene,
and it was starting to come alive beneath the skilful

strokes of her brushes when she was distracted by the sound of someone entering the cottage.

She looked up and her heart lurched joyously in her breast when she saw Chad walking into the studio. He stopped a few paces away from her and, hooking his thumbs into the snakeskin belt hugging his grey slacks to his lean hips, he observed her with a faintly mocking smile curving his sensuous mouth.

Megan's heartbeats subsided to a nervous fluttering against her ribs when a disturbing thought occurred to her. What was Chad's presence going to convey to her mother?

'Surprised to see me?' he asked, a flicker of amusement in his eyes, and she wondered for one frantic second if he had read her thoughts.

'I—I didn't expect you to—to come here,' she stammered foolishly, lowering her gaze to the blue open-necked shirt which seemed to span too tightly across his wide shoulders.

'Your mother has invited me to stay to lunch, and that's in . . .' he glanced at the gold watch strapped to his strong, lean wrist '. . . ten minutes.'

Megan looked away, hiding her surprise behind a sudden burst of activity, and dipped her brushes in a jar of turpentine, stirring them vigorously before she wiped the fine bristles on an old cloth which she used solely for that purpose.

'That looks cute,' remarked Chad as he came up behind her to study the unfinished painting on the easel, and the faint odour of his masculine cologne mingled with the smell of paint and turps, stirring her senses.

'It's not supposed to look cute,' she informed him with mock indignation as she rose from the stool to take off her paint-daubed smock. 'It's supposed to look realistic.'

'It's realistically cute,' he conceded, tongue-in-cheek.

Megan could not suppress that bubble of amused laughter rising in her throat and, flinging her smock aside, she turned to face him, but her laughter faded on a gasp when she found herself standing so close to him that she could almost feel the heat of his body against her own. Their eyes met and held for breathtaking seconds before his glance strayed boldly down to where her blue V-necked T-shirt hugged her small, firm breasts, and she could feel them swelling as if he had actually touched her.

Chad's eyes darkened with a desire that held her captive physically and emotionally when his hands circled her slender waist. She was incapable of resisting when he drew her closer, and a weakness surged into her limbs as his taut thighs brushed against her own. He lowered his head, his mouth hovering for one palpitating second above hers, and then he was tormenting her with those feather-light, sensually arousing kisses that made her cling to his shoulders while the blood flowed through her veins at a dizzying pace.

Her fingers slid into the short, dark hair at the nape of his strong neck to urge his head down to hers, and his kisses deepened instantly with a hunger to which Megan responded with a hunger of her own until she felt his hands shifting up beneath her T-shirt to stroke the soft, smooth skin at her waist. Her body ached to be touched, she could feel her nipples hardening in anticipation, but her mind warned against it, and she eased herself away from his equally aroused body before the final fragments of her control deserted her.

'If my mother is expecting us, then I think we'd better go.'

Her voice had sounded breathless and unrecognisably husky, and a faintly cynical smile touched his sensuous mouth when he released her to trail a teasing finger across her flushed cheeks.

'Yes, we'd better go before your mother launches a search party and finds her daughter in the arms of a villain like myself.'

A villain? Yes, he could be that at times, Megan thought, the flush in her cheeks deepening, and she could not look at Chad when they left the cottage and walked along the flagstone path through the sun-washed garden, but she had regained a measure of her composure by the time they reached the house.

She was not quite sure what she had expected, but lunch was not the ordeal she had imagined it might be. Peter and Vivien were perfect hosts, as always, and the conversation flowed naturally and comfortably.

They were lingering at the table over a cup of tea when Megan saw her father glance at Chad and say, 'I believe you're negotiating the purchase of a piece of land adjoining the game park.'

She looked up sharply, and her questioning glance collided briefly with Chad's across the table before he looked away to address her father.

'I was at the lawyer's office this morning, and the transfer ought to go through within a couple of weeks,' he said. 'It's not a very big piece of land, about ten acres, but it lies flush against the eastern boundary of the game park, and it's ideally situated to suit my needs.'

'Does this mean you've decided to stay on permanently at Izilwane?' Vivien questioned him, and Chad turned to her with a faintly amused smile.

'I like my job, and I like the climate.'

'It's our climate which was quite likely responsible for bringing on your bout of malaria,' Peter offered his medical opinion, and Chad smiled at him amiably.

'Thanks to you, Dr O'Brien, I have the means with which to cope with it in future.'

The telephone started ringing in the hall, and Megan got up to answer it. 'It's for you, Dad,' she told her father when she returned to the dining-room a few seconds later. 'It's someone from the hospital.'

'Oh, lord, what now?' her father groaned, excusing himself from the table to take the call.

Megan could hear him on the telephone in the hall, but she could not gauge much from his abrupt queries,

and they sat there in silence around the luncheon table
until he returned to the dining-room some moments later.

'Well, there go my hopes for a peaceful afternoon at
home,' he said, a grim look on his lean face.

'I gather you have to go out again,' Vivien remarked
with a calmness which indicated she had long ago resigned herself to the irregular comings and goings of her
husband.

'Every available doctor is needed at the hospital,' Peter
explained, shrugging himself into his jacket and gulping
down the last of his tea without resuming his seat at the
table. 'A bus carrying thirty passengers jumped the safety
rails on the mountain pass near the lumber camps, and
the ambulances are on their way to the hospital with the
injured.'

There was an understandable urgency in his manner
when he turned to leave, and Vivien excused herself from
the table to accompany him out of the house, leaving
Megan alone with Chad.

'I'm driving out to Thorndale this afternoon to take
a look at one of Frances' Brahman heifers which is in
calf,' Chad broke the contemplative silence between
them. 'Would you like to come with me and keep me
company?'

'I'd love to go with you, but I can't,' she declined his
invitation with a rueful smile. 'I'm sorry, Chad, but I
have work to do. I have three weeks in which to complete the illustrations for the children's book, and that
will mean working on it every spare moment I have.'

'Are you coming out to Izilwane on Monday?'

Megan clasped her hands nervously in her lap and
shook her head. 'I doubt it.'

'What about your curio shop?'

'Dorothy is quite capable of taking care of everything
for me while I'm away.'

The atmosphere was becoming extraordinarily tense
and strained between them. Oh, why did it have to sound

as if she was deliberately making excuses in an attempt to avoid being with him?

'When am I going to see you again?' he demanded, his narrowed glance capturing and holding hers across the table.

'I'm not sure.'

Chad flung down his table napkin and pushed back his chair to get to his feet. His features were taut and angry, and there was a hint of menace in his stride when he stepped round the table towards her.

'Confound it, Megan, I——'

He broke off abruptly at the sound of approaching footsteps, and Megan had also risen agitatedly from her chair by the time her mother came into the dining-room.

'Are you deserting us as well, Chad?' Vivien demanded, her curious glance darting from Chad to Megan and back as if she had sensed the presence of tension in the room.

'I'm afraid I must, Mrs O'Brien.' Chad answered Vivien smoothly, but the polite smile about his mouth did not reach his steel-grey eyes. 'Thank you for a delightful lunch, and I hope that some day soon I shall be able to return the invitation.'

'I'll walk with you to your car,' Megan offered hastily when he turned to leave, and she accompanied him out of the house in abject silence.

The reflection of the sun on the Porsche's windshield blinded her as they descended the steps into the driveway, and she turned her head to encounter Chad's rigid, unyielding profile. He was being unreasonable, she was thinking, and there was no need for her to apologise, but when he slid behind the wheel of his car and slammed the door shut, she found herself murmuring, 'I'm sorry, Chad.'

There was a look of cynical disbelief in the eyes that met hers as he turned the key in the ignition, and she backed away nervously as the Porsche's engine roared to life.

Chad was speeding down the circular driveway a second later, and Megan lingered out there in the scorching sun until long after his Porsche had disappeared down the street. She would have given anything to go with him, but in this instance her work had to come first. If only Chad could accept and understand that!

A helpless sigh escaped her as she turned to go indoors. Chad would have to sort out his own feelings on this matter, but she had work to do, and the sooner she got back to it, the better.

CHAPTER EIGHT

THERE WAS a refreshing coolness in the breeze that wafted into the studio through the open window, and the perfect silence of the night was disturbed only by the varying sounds of the many insects in the undergrowth. A moth circled the spotlight trained on the easel, but Megan was too absorbed in what she was doing to be aware of the insect which seemed intent on bashing itself senseless against the glass casing.

A car turned into the side street, the hum of its powerful engine becoming louder as it drew near, but she paid no attention to it until the engine was cut and the sound of a car door being slammed reached her ears. Her hand stilled, halting the delicate brush strokes on the canvas, and her stomach muscles contracted nervously when she heard heavy footsteps coming up the path towards the entrance of the cottage.

Chad? She brushed that thought aside almost the instant it entered her mind. She had neither seen him nor heard from him in almost two weeks, so why should her late-night visitor be Chad?

Megan put down her palette and brush and rose slowly to her feet to arch her aching back. She had had a difficult time trying to put Chad out of her mind to concentrate on her work, and she did not want to start thinking and wondering about him now when she was so close to completing her task.

There was a sharp knock on the door. It jarred Megan's nerves, but it was nothing compared to what she felt when she recognised Chad's tall, wide-shouldered frame beneath the porch light.

He was dressed casually in a grey, checked shirt and faded blue denims, but her heart lurched anxiously in her breast as her gaze shifted higher to his face. He looked grim and exhausted with deep shadows beneath his eyes, and compassion melted away all the anger she had stored up.

'May I come in, or are you too busy to receive visitors?' he asked, a humourless smile curving his sensuous mouth, and Megan stepped back without speaking to let him in.

The faint smell of aftershave quivered in her nostrils as he brushed past her. It teased her senses, and her legs suddenly felt shaky beneath her when she closed the door and led the way into the studio.

'Why don't you tell me I'm a selfish, unreasonable lout for behaving the way I did the last time I was here?' he demanded harshly, his fingers snaking unexpectedly about her wrist and spinning her round to face him.

'You're a selfish, unreasonable lout,' she echoed readily, and with feeling, but her pulses jerked nervously when she saw the smoky fire that leapt into his eyes.

He pulled her roughly, almost angrily, into his arms, but Megan stood rigid in his embrace as he took possession of her lips. She did not want to respond, but her lips parted beneath the sensual expertise of his mouth moving back and forth against hers, and she welcomed the invasion of his tongue as the white-hot passion of his kiss engulfed her to spread like liquid fire through her veins.

Stripped of her resistance, her body yielded to Chad's dominance, and she trembled beneath his hands when he eased her loose-fitting smock from her shoulders and down along her arms in one fluid, exciting caress. It fell to the floor at her feet, leaving her less restricted in her strapless summer frock, and her arms went up of their own volition to circle his neck when he drew her closer into the hard curve of his aroused body.

His mouth left hers to seek out the sensitive areas along her throat and shoulders, and a jerky breath passed her lips as his hands roamed her body to play havoc with her emotions. She could feel the heat of his touch burning her skin through the thin, silky material when he explored the gentle curve of her hips and thighs, and then his fingers were tugging at the bow which held the bodice of her frock firmly in place above her breasts.

Megan's hands fluttered down to his wrists to stop him when she remembered that she was not wearing a bra, but she was too late. Her silky bodice had slithered down to nestle above the belt at her waist, and a moan of pleasure escaped her when Chad's hands blazed a sensual, fiery path across her bare, responsive flesh. This was wrong, she told herself, but the desire to halt it was no longer there when she felt her body come alive to the most intoxicating sensations.

Oh, what am I doing? she wondered crazily when his probing, stroking fingers were coaxing her rosy nipples into hard, throbbing buttons of the most exquisite desire.

'I think I'm losing my heart to you, Megan,' Chad murmured throatily, his teeth nipping gently at her earlobe and sending a spate of new sensations spiralling through her.

Oh, if only that were true! Megan was thinking as she surfaced from that deep well of her own turbulent emotions to push him away from her.

'I think you're too exhausted to know what you're saying,' she replied, her voice uncommonly husky and her cheeks flaming as she lifted the bodice of her frock over her breasts and fastened the bow with unsteady fingers.

She was too afraid to look at him; too afraid of what he might see in her eyes. Her smock lay on the floor at their feet, and she stooped quickly, picking it up and flinging it carelessly across the back of a chair as she turned away from Chad. She walked towards her easel and forcibly channelled her mind towards the mundane. Her brushes needed to be cleaned before the paint dried on them, and, seeking something with which to occupy her hands, she gathered up the brushes and plunged them into a can of turps.

'You may be right,' Chad remarked laconically. 'I must be too exhausted to know what I'm saying,' he added with a faintly mocking laugh.

Dammit! Did he *have* to agree with her?

'The past two weeks have been tremendously tiring,' Chad continued without waiting for her to comment on his remark, and Megan's pulses were still throbbing at an unnatural pace when he came up beside her to stare at the painting on the easel, but she had a feeling that he was staring at it without seeing the little boy hugging his puppy. 'Between the game park and the farming community I've been kept pretty busy, and I spent most of today in and out of the Land Rover with a couple of trackers, tracking down a lion with an infected wound which had to be treated.'

A shiver of fear raced through her. She was aware of the danger involved in such an exercise where a lion had to be singled out and darted to receive the necessary treatment, but she remained silent about her fears for Chad's safety.

'I don't know what I would have done without Glenys these past two weeks.' He sighed deeply and combed his fingers through his dark hair in a tired and totally uncharacteristic gesture. 'Her assistance in the office and the surgery has been invaluable.'

'Glenys?' queried Megan, her heartbeats finally under control as she raised her bewildered glance to his.

'Glenys Gibson, my secretary.'

'Oh, yes, I'd forgotten.' She lowered her gaze hastily and removed the brushes from the can of turps to wipe them dry with unnecessary vigour, while her mind conjured up a vision of the young woman whom Chad had appointed as his secretary some weeks ago. 'She's very attractive,' she mused out aloud, but she could have bitten off her tongue the next instant when she heard Chad's throaty, mocking laughter.

'Yes, Glenys *is* rather attractive,' he agreed, arousing an unfamiliar stab of jealousy in Megan. 'I must admit I've always had a preference for tall, leggy brunettes.'

'So I've noticed,' she murmured caustically, hiding her misery behind a smile. 'The first time I saw you at Alexa and Revil Bradstone's home you were accompanied by a tall, leggy brunette.'

'Your memory of that meeting is obviously better than mine, but that was in the past.' The brushes and the cloth were removed unceremoniously from her hands, and the mockery was still there in his smile as he turned her into his arms. 'At the moment I have a definite preference for small, slender young women with honey-gold hair, and soft, inviting lips.'

'Flattery will get you nowhere!'

'I have yet to meet a woman who doesn't respond to flattery,' he insisted with a derisive laugh, lowering his head to hers, but she evaded his seeking mouth and raised her hands to place them flat against his hard chest.

'Sit down,' she instructed, giving him a none too gentle push on to the leather couch behind him. 'I'll go and make us a cup of coffee.'

He did not follow her into the small kitchen, and Megan was intensely relieved to have those few moments to herself to gather her scattered wits about her. She would have to be a great deal more cautious in future where Chad was concerned if she did not want him to guess how she felt about him. It was painful enough to love him and to know that he could never love her in return, but his mockery and his contempt would drive her beyond the limit of her endurance.

Chad was standing with his fingers pushed deep into the back pockets of his denims when Megan returned to the studio with their coffee. He was admiring the completed paintings which she had propped up against the wall beneath the open window, and he turned to take the mug of coffee she offered him, his glance thoughtful.

'You must have worked day and night these past two weeks to complete all these paintings.'

'Almost,' she smiled up at him, and a teasing light entered his steel-grey eyes.

'You're an artist who knows how to apply realism to your work, but I still think that "cute" is the best way to describe these illustrations,' he said, making himself comfortable on the leather couch and stretching his long, muscular legs out in front of him, and this time Megan did not contradict his observation as she lowered herself on to the stool in front of the easel.

Chad questioned her in detail about her work while they drank their coffee, and she would have liked to believe that his interest was genuine. Art, in any form or style, was Megan's favourite topic of conversation. She could talk about it for hours without tiring of the subject, but she was wary of Chad's mockery, and she limited herself solely to answering his questions.

'What do you plan to do with that piece of land you bought?' she asked, changing the subject as she took his empty mug from him and placed it on the low, circular table beside her stool.

'I haven't given it much thought lately.' His tired features creased with a suggestion of a smile as he studied the tips of his grey, suede shoes. 'The bungalow is comfortable, but I can't stay there for an unspecified length of time, so I might build a house on that land adjoining the game park and settle down.'

Megan was in the grip of a sudden and inexplicable tension when a moth darted down between them only to swoop up again towards the spotlight. The sound of its wings fluttering against the glass casing shattered that brief, intense silence in the room, but it also jarred her nerves, and forced her to pull herself together.

'When a man talks about settling down it usually means that he's thinking of getting married and having a family, but for you it must mean something quite the opposite,' she observed drily, lacing her fingers together in her lap.

'Hm . . . yes.' His smile deepened with mockery. 'I've been considering the possibility of starting my own private harem.'

'That sounds true to form,' she laughed mirthlessly, and Chad's eyes narrowed to speculative slits.

'If I offered you the position of first lady of the harem, would you accept?'

'No, I wouldn't, thank you very much,' she responded stiffly.

'Pity,' he murmured, his mouth curving in a lazy, sensuous smile. 'You're a power-house of suppressed passion, which I have every intention of exploring at some future date because I believe we'd be good together.'

A wave of embarrassed heat surged into Megan's cheeks, and she lowered her gaze hastily. 'I'm sorry I started this conversation.'

'I'm not.'

Chad was enjoying her discomfiture, and she could almost hate him for it when everything inside her seemed to be caught up in a vice of misery. 'It's getting late,' she said, rising jerkily to her feet.

'Yes, it's getting late, and you want to get on with your work,' he announced with a surprising amiability as he drew in his feet and stood up. 'When are you returning to Izilwane?'

'Next Monday,' she replied, her back turned resolutely towards him until she had time to school her features, but Chad's hands were on her shoulders, his touch setting fire to her skin as he turned her relentlessly to face him.

'Perhaps we could meet for lunch in the restaurant on Monday,' he suggested, his glance a warm, exciting caress trailing across the delicate contours of her face and lingering on her soft, quivering mouth.

'I'd like that,' she managed, the suffocating pace of her heart making it difficult to speak.

Chad's hands tightened on her shoulders, warning her of his intentions, but her treacherous limbs refused to obey the messages relayed from her brain, and she found herself trapped helplessly against the length of his hard male body. His warm mouth shifted over hers, stifling her protests and demanding a response from her which she was determined to withhold, but her resistance crumbled once again like a house of cards collapsing in the breeze.

'You frighten me, Chad,' she whispered shakily when he finally eased his mouth from hers.

She buried her flushed face against his broad chest, inhaling the clean male smell of him and hating herself for being so weak, but his fingers were beneath her chin, forcing her to look at him.

'You have nothing to fear, Megan.' Mockery mingled with the smoky desire in those pale grey eyes probing hers. 'I gave you my word that I wouldn't push you into something which you're not ready for, but that doesn't stop me wanting to hold you and kiss you and touch you ... like this.'

His demonstration left her breathless and trembling and more than a little dishevelled. 'I doubt if I shall ever be ready for what you have in mind,' she said, restoring a certain amount of order to her appearance, but her treacherous body was saying exactly the opposite.

'I know I can make you want me, and that's a start.'

Megan could not argue with that. Chad had the ability to make her want him, and she could so very easily give herself to him, but in doing so she knew she would be following that road which led to nowhere.

'I think you'd better go,' she whispered, her aching throat warning her that she was perilously close to tears, and the last thing she wanted was to weep in front of Chad.

A muscle leapt in his jaw, and his sensuous mouth tightened into a thin, hard line. 'You're right, I'd better go.'

He turned on his heel, striding out of the studio, and Megan followed him in silence. He was angry, and so was she, but her anger was directed at fate for making her fall in love with a man who would simply use her and cast her aside.

'I'll see you at lunch on Monday, and we'll make that one o'clock,' he said, his expression inscrutable when he met her glance for a brief moment.

'I'll be there,' she promised, and then he was striding out to where he had parked his Porsche beneath the street light.

Megan closed the door after he had driven away and returned to her studio with its familiar smell of paint and turps. For some obscure reason she felt emotionally raw and bruised, and she sat down heavily on the stool in front of the easel to stare at the half-finished painting on the easel. The carefree laughter on the children's faces seemed to mock her ruthlessly, and a terrifying wave of pain and helpless rage surged through her.

'Oh, why did it have to be Chad?' she groaned, closing her eyes in a physical attempt to shut out the pain searing through her. 'If I had to fall in love, then why couldn't it have been with someone less complicated?'

She sighed tiredly and draped a cloth over the painting on the easel. It was futile to think she could continue where she had left off earlier that evening when Chad arrived. Her mental rhythm had been disrupted, and all she wanted at that moment was to curl up somewhere to mourn the loss of something which never had, and never would, belong to her.

Megan's return to Izilwane was delayed. Her car refused to start on the Monday morning. The engine coughed and spluttered when she turned the key in the ignition, and then it simply petered out. It seemed to take ages before the mechanic arrived with the tow truck and, after a brief inspection of the Mazda's engine, Megan was warned that the repairs might take several hours.

'It's important that I have my car returned to me by twelve-thirty,' she wailed anxiously at the mechanic, remembering her luncheon appointment with Chad.

'We'll do our best, Miss O'Brien,' he promised before he towed her Mazda away.

Megan spent the morning pacing the floor in agitation and, much to her mother's amusement, she was all but chewing her fingernails when the telephone rang at noon that day.

'We apologise for the delay, Miss O'Brien,' said the workshop manager. 'We had difficulty in finding the fault, but your car will be delivered to you at one o'clock sharp.'

Megan had never felt so frustrated in all her life. She wanted to scream, but she knew it would not help, and she merely thanked the workshop manager politely before she replaced the receiver.

'What do I do *now*?' she asked of no one in particular.

'I don't know why you've been in such a hellish rush all morning to return to Izilwane.' Vivien eyed her daughter reprovingly. 'You know you have nothing to worry about while you have Dorothy to take care of things for you in the shop.'

Megan told her mother the truth out of sheer frustration. 'I have a luncheon appointment at one o'clock with Chad.'

'Oh, I see.' Vivien's expression cleared with understanding. 'Well, in that case, you'd better let Chad know that you've been unavoidably delayed.'

'He now has a private line to his office in the veterinary building, and I don't have his number.'

'The telecommunication department at the Post Office will give you his number.'

Of course! Megan could have kicked herself at that moment. If she had not been so rattled she might have thought of that herself, and she calmed herself with an effort.

'I'm afraid Dr McAdam isn't in the building at the moment,' Chad's secretary informed her a few minutes later in her charmingly husky voice. 'May I know who is speaking?'

'Megan O'Brien.'

There was a brief pause, then Glenys Gibson said, 'Could I give him a message, Miss O'Brien?'

'Yes, please.' Megan brushed aside her disappointment and hastily collected her thoughts. 'I would appreciate it if you would tell him that I've had problems with my car, and that I'll be a little late for our luncheon appointment.'

'I'll pass on your message as soon as Dr McAdam comes in,' Glenys assured her, and Megan sighed audibly as she put down the phone.

'You can relax now.'

Megan smiled at her mother, but she knew she would not relax entirely until she was seated across the table from Chad.

The Mazda was delivered to the house in the stifling heat at one o'clock 'sharp' as the workshop manager had promised, and fifteen minutes later, hot and irritated by the fact that she was late, Megan was entering the restaurant at Izilwane where the air-conditioning enfolded her like a cool, refreshing breeze.

Isaac came instantly to her aid. 'May I show you to a table, Miss Megan?'

Megan nodded, her eager glance sweeping across the crowded restaurant in search of Chad. 'I'm meeting Dr McAdam for lunch.'

'Dr McAdam is not here. He had a cup of coffee and left a few minutes ago.'

That's odd! thought Megan, her heart skipping an anxious beat as she turned to meet Isaac's curious glance. 'Did he say he was coming back?'

Isaac shook his head. 'He never said anything, Miss Megan. He drank his coffee and then he left.'

'Perhaps he was called away,' she suggested hopefully, but Isaac shook his head once again.

'There was no call for him while he was here.'

Megan was confused and troubled. It showed on her face and she hovered with indecision before she murmured, 'Thank you, Isaac,' and turned to leave.

'What about lunch, Miss Megan?' Isaac called after her, but she waved it aside.

'I'll have something later.'

She went in search of Chad. He would not have walked out on their luncheon appointment without leaving a message unless something was seriously wrong, and she had a feeling it was important to discover the reason behind his odd behaviour. He was not in his bungalow, and the veterinary building was deserted. Half an hour later Megan had to relinquish her search when no one seemed to know where she might find Chad, and anxiety and tension sat like a lead weight in her chest when she eventually sought the air-conditioned sanctuary of the curio shop.

She skipped lunch that day. She was too upset to think about ordering something from the restaurant when she sat down behind her desk and stared at the pile of paperwork which needed her urgent attention. Time had been her enemy that day, and she clenched her hands on the desk in frustration. Why hadn't Chad *waited*?

She somehow managed to set her personal problems aside to draw the stack of papers towards her and, with Dorothy attending to the customers, she waded systematically through the documents and letters which had accumulated on her desk during her absence.

Megan received a call from the railway station in Louisville to inform her that a batch of parcels had arrived on the midday train, but it was late that afternoon before she could leave the shop to make the necessary arrangements for the collection of those parcels.

Bill Hadley's office was situated in the administrative section adjoining the main building, and Megan was walking across the deserted pool area when she saw Chad's khaki-clad frame leaving Bill's office with those long, lithe strides she knew so well.

Her smile was welcoming as he approached her, the words 'I've been worried about you' leaping to her tongue, but they froze on her parting lips when his cold, contemptuous eyes made stabbing contact with hers before he looked away as if she did not exist. Megan stood transfixed, red flags of humiliation searing her cheeks when he strode past her on his way to the main building, and then the blood receded slowly and painfully from her face to leave her deathly pale.

Her pain and confusion were mirrored in her eyes as she watched the glass doors swing shut behind Chad. She was shaking like a leaf, and several agonising seconds elapsed before she managed to regain a fraction of her composure.

She had been snubbed, but she could not imagine why. What had she done to deserve being hurt and humiliated in this way?

Megan faced Bill Hadley across his desk a few minutes later, making the necessary arrangements for the parcels to be collected at the railway station. She was having difficulty with her concentration, and if she conducted her business in a faintly distracted manner, then Bill was tactful enough not to mention it.

She returned to the shop in time to see Dorothy off before she tidied up her desk and locked up. The shock of what had occurred had worn off, but the pain and humiliation still lingered like a thorn embedded deep beneath the skin, and Megan knew that she could not leave the matter there. She intended to confront Chad that same evening, and she would demand an explanation for the abominable way she had been treated.

The telephone started ringing just as she was about to leave the shop, and she dashed back into her office to snatch up the receiver. She nursed a vague hope that it might be Chad, but it was Byron, and his news made her realise she would have to postpone her intended confrontation with Chad.

Frances had given birth to their child, a boy, earlier that afternoon, and Byron was offering Megan the opportunity to drive into town with him that evening to visit her cousin in hospital.

'Congratulations, Byron!' Megan laughed elatedly, thrusting her problems aside for the moment. 'I'm so happy for both of you, and I would appreciate a lift into town to meet the new addition to the family.'

'I'm in desperate need of a shower and a change of clothing, but I'll be at your bungalow in thirty minutes to pick you up,' he told her before he ended their brief conversation.

Megan's sombre, unhappy mood shifted aside like a dark, heavy cloud which had been obscuring the warmth of the sun, and her heart felt considerably lighter when, half an hour later, she was seated beside Byron in his expensive BMW, speeding through the dusk to Louisville. The birth of Byron and Frances' baby son was creating an exciting and much-needed diversion, and Chad's humiliating snub was eased temporarily from her mind.

'Have you decided on a name for the baby?' she questioned Byron during the fifteen-minute drive into town.

'We want to call him Daniel.' Byron glanced at her briefly, and there was pride in the smile he flashed at her. 'It's a name we both like, and it also happens to be my late father's name.'

'Daniel,' she echoed softly, smiling as she savoured the name. 'I like it,' she said at length, looking forward to seeing the baby as she stared straight ahead of her at the BMW's twin beams piercing the swiftly gathering darkness of night. 'Yes, I like it very much.'

Frances was sitting up in bed, gazing down at the baby in her arms with a look of incredulous wonder on her face when they walked into her private ward in the hospital's maternity section. Her raven-black hair was tied back with a blue scarf into the nape of her neck, and her dark eyes were warm and misty with happiness when she raised her face for Byron's kiss.

A look of tender devotion passed between Byron and Frances as he seated himself on the bed beside her and draped an arm about her shoulders. Megan had witnessed that look, and her throat tightened with envy, but she swallowed down that uncomfortable lump when she stepped forward to plant a congratulatory kiss on Frances' cheek.

'Isn't he beautiful, Megan?' her cousin wanted to know.

'Beautiful,' echoed Megan, drawing aside the baby blanket to get a clearer view of the tiny infant sleeping contentedly in his mother's arms.

His hair was dark, and the small, pink face was wrinkled and puffy, but he *was* beautiful. Megan trailed her fingers lightly across one soft cheek, and a wave of despair engulfed her as, for the first time in her life, she knew an intense longing to have a home and a family of her own, but it was a dream which she knew would have to remain a dream forever.

'I'm glad you were free to come here this evening.' Frances scattered her distressing thoughts. 'There's something Byron and I would like to ask you.'

Megan glanced at their grave features and a nervous smile plucked at her mouth. 'This sounds serious.'

'It is serious.' Frances glanced at Byron, but he gestured that she should continue. 'It would make our happiness complete if you would agree to be Daniel's godmother,' she explained. 'Would you, Megan?'

A warmth invaded Megan's cold, aching heart, and her eyes misted with tears. 'I'm honoured that you should ask me, and I accept gladly.'

They were all, momentarily, too emotional to speak, then Frances said, 'Would you like to hold your godson?'

'I was beginning to think I'd have to wait until you're home on the farm to hold him,' Megan laughed shakily, taking the small, precious bundle from her cousin.

This was the closest she was going to get to having a child of her own, she was thinking as she cradled little Daniel Rockford in her arms, but she was not going to allow this moment of happiness to be tainted with sadness, and she banished her dismal thoughts as she lowered her head to brush her lips lightly against the baby's small, warm forehead.

Later that evening, when Megan was alone in her bungalow at Izilwane, the events of the day closed in on her with a vengeance, and her joy dwindled, leaving her the pain and humiliation of Chad's rebuff to contend with.

Chad's bungalow had been in darkness when she had returned from the hospital, but it was shortly after ten that evening, when she was making herself a cup of tea in her kitchen, that she saw the lights go on in his lounge. Should she wait until morning, or should she go and see him now?

She decided on the latter when she saw him moving about in his lounge through the gap in the curtains at the window. There was no sense in delaying it, she told herself as she switched off the kettle and took a pace towards the door, but the next instant she halted abruptly.

Chad was not alone in his bungalow. Glenys Gibson was there, and she was standing close to him, saying something and smiling up at him provocatively while he put an arm about her waist and led her away from the window.

The pain that tore through Megan was like the savage twist of a knife in a raw wound, and she groaned out aloud in agony as she slumped back against the wall beside the kitchen door. She could imagine where Chad was taking that tall, leggy brunette, and she raised her trembling hands to her face, covering her eyes in an almost childish attempt to shut out the mental visions of Chad making love to Glenys Gibson, but her tortured mind was cruelly persistent.

'Oh, help me!' she groaned in anguish, plunging her bungalow into darkness, and stumbling into her bedroom to fling herself across her bed with its patchwork quilt.

She was shivering despite the warmth of the night, and the pain that stabbed at her insides finally subsided to leave her mercifully numb. She had known from the start that it would be fatal to become emotionally involved with a man like Chad McAdam, and she had only herself to blame for the pain and misery she would have to endure for the rest of her life.

There was one thing, however, which she could not leave undone. She could not go on without knowing the reason behind his rude snub and, if necessary, she would apologise for whatever it was she was supposed to have done. That way their fragile relationship would at least end on an amicable basis.

CHAPTER NINE

MEGAN had lain awake most of the night, tormented by her thoughts, and in the end she had overslept. The face that met hers in the bathroom mirror that Tuesday morning was pale and pinched with dark shadows beneath the eyes, and she was nursing a nagging headache when she finally arrived at the shop at a quarter to nine.

Dorothy was attending to the customers browsing among the shelves and showcases in search of souvenirs, and Megan managed to slip through into her office almost without being seen. She searched her desk drawers for the tablets she always kept there, and she gulped down two with a glass of water. She leaned against her desk with her eyes closed, feeling guilty about arriving late, but there was something she had to do which could not wait, and that meant she would have to leave Dorothy in charge of the shop a while longer.

She turned to leave her office, her movements hurried with the need to put this nerve-racking task behind her, but the next instant the breath was almost knocked from her lungs as she collided heavily with a hard, khaki-clad body in the doorway. Strong hands steadied her, but her own hands had gone out instinctively to clutch at tautly muscled arms, and she knew it was Chad long before she raised her wary glance to encounter his handsome, granite-hard features.

'I was on my way to see you,' she croaked, recovering her breath with difficulty and breaking free of his hands to back away from him.

Chad's cold-eyed, cynical-mouthed expression chilled Megan, and there was a hint of menace in his manner when he stepped into her cupboard-sized office and closed the door firmly behind him. 'I was inexcusably

140

rude to you yesterday, and I owe you an apology,' he said, 'but I'd also like to thank you for bringing me to my senses.'

The room suddenly seemed airless, and Megan was convinced that her headache was getting worse instead of better as she stared up at him with bewilderment in her cornflower-blue eyes.

'I—I don't know what you mean,' she stammered, cringing inwardly beneath the icy contempt in those eyes raking her body as if they wanted to rid her of more than her pink checked blouse and white slacks.

'I was beginning to think that you're different, Megan, but you're not, and I'm grateful to you for strengthening my belief that no woman can be trusted—not even to keep a luncheon appointment.'

Megan staggered mentally beneath the impact of his statement, but her understanding of the situation was swift and sharp. Chad had not received her message, and that was why she had been subjected to that humiliating snub the day before, but to confront him with the truth could create problems of a different nature. She did not want that, but she knew she had no choice when he turned to leave her office.

'Just a minute!' She clutched at his arm to stop him before he could open the door, and she felt the muscles tensing beneath her fingers when he turned back to her with a look of such icy disdain on his face that her courage almost deserted her completely. 'Now that you've had your say, I would appreciate it if you would allow me to have mine,' she said, removing her hand hastily from his arm and facing him with a calmness she was far from experiencing. 'I was delayed yesterday because my car developed a mechanical fault which took hours to repair. I arrived fifteen minutes late for our appointment, but by that time you'd already left the restaurant.'

A look of cynical disbelief flashed across Chad's lean face, and he smiled twistedly. 'Am I supposed to accept that explanation as the truth?'

Megan was not accustomed to having her word doubted, and she felt that familiar stab of anger which only Chad could arouse in her, but she forced herself to remain outwardly cool and calm.

'Please feel free to check up on what I've told you.' She despised herself for the noticeable tremor in her hand when she reached for the telephone on her desk and held the receiver out to him. 'If you phone the garage in town they'll confirm that they delivered my car to me at one o'clock, and Isaac will tell you that I arrived at the restaurant about fifteen minutes later.'

'You could have called to let me know you'd be late,' he argued harshly, releasing his grip on the door handle and snatching the receiver from her hand to slam it back on to its cradle with a savage force that made her flinch. 'I was out for most of the morning, but Glenys was in the office, and you could have left a message with her.'

Megan's nerves had coiled into an aching knot at the pit of her stomach, and her vague, nagging headache had progressed to a savagely painful throbbing against her temples. This was the moment she had dreaded. She could try subterfuge, but one look at the angry features of the man who stood towering over her made her realise that only the truth would suffice.

'I did leave a message,' she confessed in a voice just above a whisper. 'It must have been mislaid.'

A look of cold fury shifted into his eyes. 'Glenys is not in the habit of mislaying messages.'

'I'm sure she isn't,' Megan agreed, trying desperately to remain calm, 'and I'm not attempting to discredit her to you, but for some reason she must have mislaid the message I left for you.'

'Name one reason why I should believe you, and it had better be good!' he challenged, his lips drawn back against his teeth in a snarl and his angry eyes glinting like flints of steel as they blazed down into hers.

'I'll give you two reasons,' she responded to his challenge. 'I didn't have your telephone number, and I had to call the Post Office telecommunications department to get it. If you need to have that verified, then I'll give you the name of the man I spoke to. Secondly, my mother was standing beside me when I called your office, and she will confirm that I left a message with your secretary.'

A deafening silence settled in the room, and Megan wondered if Chad could hear the heavy, anxious beat of her heart as they stood there facing each other with less than a pace between them.

'I believe you,' he said eventually, oddly white about the mouth when he turned from her to frown at the calendar hanging against the wall, and relief washed over Megan with a force that made her want to weep.

'Thank you,' she murmured shakily.

'Lord, this is *damnable*!' he growled, passing an agitated hand over his hair and letting his fingers rest for a moment at the nape of his neck before he dropped his hand to his side.

'I'm glad we could clear up this misunderstanding.'

Megan's legs were trembling and threatening to cave in beneath her, but she leaned heavily against the desk and remained standing when Chad turned to her with a mixture of anger and frustration etched sharply on his chiselled features. 'We've got to talk, Megan. We've got to do something about eliminating these trivial misunderstandings, but I'm leaving for Johannesburg as soon as I've had a chat with Byron, and I won't be back until next Monday.'

'We may pass each other on the way,' Megan enlightened him coolly, not sure that she wanted to have this *talk* with him. 'I have to take my illustrations through to the publishers in Johannesburg on Monday, and I shan't be returning until the Wednesday.'

'I've got an idea.' Chad smiled faintly, and Megan gripped the edge of the desk behind her for added support when he lessened the distance between them. 'My company's plane is flying up some veterinary equipment for me first thing Monday morning, and it would be no problem at all for me to arrange that you be a passenger on the return trip to Johannesburg. I'll delay my departure until the Wednesday morning, and then we'll drive back together.'

That might have all the ingredients of a sensible suggestion, but Megan was beginning to feel like an animal edged into a trap from which there would be no escape.

'I appreciate your kind offer, Chad, but I don't think it would be——'

'Think it over and let me know,' he cut in persuasively, drawing the small notepad on her desk towards him and using her pen to scribble a row of figures on it. 'This is my private telephone number at Aztec. I'm not sure of my time schedule during the next few days, but you can reach me at my office on Sunday evening.'

'Chad, I really don't think I can——'

'Don't decline my offer in such haste,' he cut in once again, straightening to place silencing fingers against her lips when she persisted with her protests. 'Promise me you'll at least think it over?'

Robbed of the strength to argue with him while his fingers trailed fire across her jaw, she whispered, 'I promise.'

Chad tipped her face up to his and kissed her briefly on the lips before he turned to open the door and, raising his hand to his forehead in a mock salute, he walked out of her office and out of the shop.

Megan collapsed weakly on to her chair, and her heart was still beating much too hard and fast for comfort when she looked up to see Dorothy hovering anxiously in the doorway.

'Are you all right, Miss Megan?' she asked, and Megan pulled herself together sharply to smile reassuringly at her assistant.

'Yes, thank you, Dorothy. Everything's OK.'

'I didn't like the look on Dr McAdam's face when he walked into your office and closed the door, and I don't mind telling you I was worried.'

'There was a private matter which needed to be settled between Dr McAdam and myself,' Megan explained, and Dorothy stared intently at her hollow-eyed features before she nodded and turned away to attend to the customer who had walked into the shop.

Megan stared at the telephone number which Chad had written down on her small notepad. Should she accept his offer, or would it be wiser to decline? She was still too shaky in mind and body to make that decision now and, ripping the sheet of paper out of the notepad, she folded it neatly and slipped it into her handbag.

As the day progressed her energy flagged. By four-thirty that afternoon she was thinking seriously about suggesting to Dorothy that they close up shop and go home, but she was still considering that possibility when the telephone rang on her desk, and she sighed inwardly as she lifted the receiver to her ear.

'Megan O'Brien speaking.'

'I hope I'm not calling at an inconvenient time, Miss O'Brien. It's Glenys Gibson.'

The introduction had been unnecessary. Megan had a good ear for voices, and Glenys Gibson's attractively husky voice was not one she was likely to forget in a hurry.

'What can I do for you, Miss Gibson?'

'I was wondering if you could meet me in the Ladies' Bar just after five this evening for a drink and a chat.'

Megan wished she could decline the invitation. She had been looking forward to going home to her bunga-low to relax in a hot bath before she made herself a quick snack and crawled into bed, but something warned her that this meeting with Glenys Gibson was more important than succumbing to her desire for an early night.

'I'll meet you there at five,' she answered her curtly, replacing the receiver and admitting to herself that curiosity had been the deciding factor. What was there that Glenys Gibson could possibly want to talk to her about?

The Ladies' Bar with its wood-panelled walls and soft lighting was a favourite gathering place during the peak season in the game park, but on this particular evening it was practically deserted, and Megan was already seated in a comfortable armchair when Glenys Gibson joined her.

Glenys was an attractive young woman with shoulder-length hair and jade-green eyes surrounded by dark, incredibly long lashes, but Megan could not help noticing that her smile was tinged with nervousness when they sat facing each other across the low, circular table. The steward approached their table, and Glenys ordered a gin and tonic while Megan chose a non-alcoholic glass of soda with a dash of lime.

They discussed the bushveld heat which was still predominant even though winter was practically on their doorstep, and they discussed several other unimportant matters, but Glenys came straight to the point when their drinks arrived.

'I owe you an apology,' she said, swallowing down a mouthful of her drink and nursing her glass between her slender, manicured hands. 'I didn't forget to pass on your message to Chad. It was deliberate.'

Megan's insides went into a spasm. It had never crossed her mind that Glenys's lapse had been deliberate, and the truth left her momentarily at a loss for words.

'If our positions had been reversed I know I'd have been as angry as hell,' Glenys continued, 'and I wouldn't blame you if you let rip with a few choice words.'

Am I angry? No. Hurt and confused, maybe, but not angry, Megan analysed her feelings.

'You could have remained silent and I would never have known, but you had the courage to confront me with the truth, and I admire you for that.' Megan sipped at her drink to moisten her dry mouth, and she wished now that she had asked for something stronger than soda water and lime when she felt her insides quiver in the aftermath of shock. 'Have you told Chad?'

'No.' There was anxiety in the jade-green eyes that met Megan's. 'Are *you* going to tell him?'

'No,' Megan replied without hesitation, and Glenys Gibson's features relaxed visibly.

'Thank you,' she murmured with a shaky smile, raising her glass to her crimson lips and sipping her gin and tonic while she eyed Megan curiously. 'Don't you want to know why I didn't give him your message?'

'I'm sure you must have had a very good reason for not passing on my message, but I don't consider it any of my business.'

'You really are quite something, aren't you?' Glenys's green gaze was incredulous, and then a look of determination shifted across her face. 'Look, you may not particularly want to hear this, and I apologise for taking up so much of your time, but I know I won't feel better until I've made a full confession.'

Megan was not sure that she wanted to hear more, but she could not deny this woman something which was of obvious importance to her, and she answered Glenys with a calmness that belied the turmoil inside her. 'If it will make you feel better to talk, then I have the time to listen.'

Glenys was obviously not in the habit of wasting time on trivialities, and once again she came straight to the point. 'I knew Chad in Johannesburg. He dated my older sister for a while, but I was crazy about him from the first time I saw him. I heard that he'd based himself up here in the game park, and I jumped at the chance to accompany my parents when they decided to move up to Louisville. Getting the job as Chad's secretary brought

me a step closer to making my dream a reality, but I
soon discovered that *you* stood in my way, and when
the opportunity presented itself to cause a rift between
you—I took it.'

The naked truth hit Megan like a shuddering blow,
rendering her speechless once again, and Glenys lowered
her lashes guiltily, but she did not spare herself as she
continued with her explanation.

'Chad worked until late last night in the laboratory.
He had to run a few important tests, and, since I was
in no hurry to leave, I hung around to take down notes
and make myself generally useful. Afterwards he invited
me to his bungalow for a nightcap. We talked and flirted
a little, but when he realised that I was angling for more
he made it painfully clear that he wasn't interested.'

A dull red colour had surged into Glenys's cheeks, but
it subsided just as swiftly, and Megan hated herself for
experiencing a sense of relief at someone else's expense.

'This morning, just before Chad left for
Johannesburg, he gave me a dressing down for not passing on your message. He was in a pretty violent mood,
and he said a few things that made me grow up in a
hurry. I've been an idiot all these years to think that I
was in love with him when, in actual fact, I was simply
clinging to my childish infatuation. It's you he wants,
and I should have known that nothing I could do would
change that.'

It's you he wants! Megan shrank inwardly as those
words echoed through her mind. She knew what Chad
wanted. He wanted her body, but she was not prepared
to give herself to a man who would give her nothing in
return.

'I've been feeling absolutely rotten about what I did,'
Glenys went on, finishing her drink and frowning down
at her glass when the ice slid to the bottom with a tink-
ling sound. 'I'm not by nature a nasty, vicious person,
but I've come to my senses where Chad McAdam is con-

cerned, and that's why I felt I owed it to you to tell you the truth—to apologise.'

Megan could not help feeling sorry for Glenys, and her smile was sympathetic. 'I understand.'

Their contemplative glances met and held and, from the debris of past errors, a mutual liking and respect was born between them.

'I can see now what it is about you that appeals to Chad. It isn't just your looks, it's your integrity, your compassion, and your capacity for understanding.' Glenys smiled rucfully. 'What he still needs to learn is that he can trust you, but trusting a woman will never come easy to a man as cynical as Chad McAdam.'

Glenys's observation had been stabbingly accurate. Chad's trust in women had been shattered at an early age, and Megan doubted if he would ever again trust a woman entirely. It saddened and angered her when she thought of how Chad's father had unwisely nurtured that lack of trust by allowing his own bitterness and cynicism to spill over on to his son.

Megan saw a movement out of the corner of her eye, and she turned her head to see Jack Harriman's lean, khaki-clad frame entering the Ladies' Bar. His sandy-coloured hair lay in its usual disorderly manner across his broad forehead, and he was smiling as he approached their table.

'May I join you?' he asked, his blue gaze going from one to the other, and it was Glenys who answered him.

'Please do join us, Jack.'

'It's been a long, hot day, and I could do with a cold beer,' he said, lowering himself into a vacant chair and gesturing to the steward. 'What about you ladies? Could I buy you another drink?'

'Nothing for me, thank you, Jack,' Megan declined hastily. 'I'll finish what I have here, and then I must leave.'

'What about you, Glenys?' he asked, and Glenys seemed to hesitate for a moment before she smiled and nodded.

'I wouldn't mind another gin and tonic.'

'A beer for me, please, Sam, and a gin and tonic for the lady here.' The steward left to place their order at the bar and Jack glanced at Megan and Glenys as he settled back comfortably in his chair. 'Have you two ladies got partners for this evening?'

'What's happening this evening that requires a partner?' Glenys demanded curiously.

'We've got our local band playing in the restaurant this evening, and it's going to be a night of wining, dining and dancing,' Jack explained, shifting his dusty boots beneath the low table where they were hidden from sight.

'Count me out,' Megan intervened. 'I'm going to have an early night.'

Jack looked at the attractive brunette and smiled. 'Would you consider being my partner for the evening, Glenys?'

Megan was aware of a certain urgency beneath the surface of his casual invitation, and she silently willed Glenys to accept when she saw her hesitate.

'I'd like that very much, thank you,' Glenys finally answered him with a hint of shyness in her smile.

'Wonderful!' he exclaimed. 'I'll call for you at seven, if that would suit you?'

'Seven would be fine,' Glenys nodded.

'If you two will excuse me, then I really must go,' Megan announced, rising from her chair and smiling into jade-green eyes across the low table. 'Thanks for the drink, Glenys, and I hope you both enjoy your evening.'

The sun was setting beyond the ridge of distant hills, casting a pink hue across the sky when she left the Ladies' Bar and walked the short distance to her bungalow. She paused briefly on her *stoep* to watch a hadeda ibis swooping low overhead as it flew to roost with its 'ha-

ha-ha-dahah' call echoing across the silent bushveld, and she sighed tiredly as she entered her bungalow.

If only life could be as simple and uncomplicated as nature! she was thinking when she closed the door behind her.

Megan had a valid reason for driving out to Thorndale on Sunday afternoon. Frances had returned home the day before with her baby, and Megan wanted to make her a gift of the landscape painting she had completed. The true reason for her visit to the farm was a restlessness brought on by indecision, but that was something she would keep to herself.

'This is magnificent, Megan!' Frances voiced her opinion as she studied the watercolour painting of willow trees trailing their branches in a winding river against the backdrop of a rocky-ridged mountain. 'You did the preliminary sketch for this painting that afternoon when you and Chad rode out to the river, didn't you?'

'Yes,' Megan nodded, looking away hastily to hide the pain and despair in her eyes.

She did not need Frances to remind her of that particular afternoon when she had been coerced into taking Chad along on that ride down to the river. The memory of it had haunted her every moment while she had worked on that painting. She had known then that Chad had the ability to disrupt her calm, comfortable existence, but she had foolishly ignored all the warnings her rational mind had issued.

'This was worth waiting for,' Frances announced, hugging her delightedly, 'and I insist that you stay and have supper with us this evening.'

Megan did not decline the invitation. The mere thought of having to return to the loneliness of her bungalow filled her with dread, but she wondered afterwards if it would not have been preferable to having to pretend to her family that nothing was amiss.

She lingered in the nursery that evening with Frances after little Daniel had been bathed, fed, and settled in his cradle. He went to sleep almost immediately, and still they lingered, marvelling at his minute perfection until Byron returned from the Grove, where he kept an excellent herd of Afrikaner cattle.

'I was hoping to be back a little earlier, but we had problems with the borehole pump,' he explained with a grimace as he hugged Frances to his broad chest and peered into the cradle at his sleeping son. 'I'm starving,' he said at length. 'What's for supper?'

'I'm not sure, but knowing Gladys, you could expect another four-course meal,' Frances replied, a humorous twinkle in her dark eyes as she disengaged herself from her husband's arm to lead the way down the passage and across the hall into the dining-room where Gladys, the buxom, elderly black woman, was checking that everything was in order with the array of sliced cold meats and salads she had set on the table.

'*Sawubona*, Miss Megan.' A white-toothed smile split her black face, but her dark eyes were critical when they flicked over Megan's small, slender frame. 'You are getting too thin, it's true,' she said in her heavily accented English. 'Maybe you must come and visit *kaningi* times, then I can put meat on your bones with my cooking.'

'Maybe I will come more often in future,' Megan smiled at her affectionately, and Gladys nodded as if the matter was settled before she left the room and returned to the kitchen, her weight making the floorboards shudder beneath her.

'Gladys was right,' observed Byron, his tawny gaze sliding over Megan's slight figure as they seated themselves at the table. 'You have lost weight.'

Megan tensed inwardly. 'I've been expending a lot of energy on my work lately.'

Byron accepted this explanation with an understanding nod and helped himself to the food on the table, but Frances continued to stare contemplatively at Megan.

'You're not ill, are you?' she asked, a worried frown creasing her smooth brow. 'You do have a rather drawn look about the eyes.'

'There's nothing wrong with me that a good night's rest won't cure,' Megan assured her cousin with a smile which she hoped would look convincing, and to her relief Frances left the matter there.

Megan tried to participate in the conversation at the supper table, but her mind wandered relentlessly. What was she going to tell Chad? Should she accept his offer, or should she reject it?

Later, when they drank their coffee out on the cool, dark veranda, she was still searching frantically for a solution to her problem, and she was beginning to despair when Byron excused himself to retire to his study. What am I going to do? she asked herself as she rose agitatedly from her chair on the veranda to lean against the wooden railings. The familiar sound and smell of the bushveld at night was all around her as she stared up at the star-studded sky, but she neither heard nor saw anything while she battled with her indecision.

'That's the third time in the last half-hour that you've jumped up out of your chair like a jack-in-the-box. Honestly, Megan, you're as restless as a horse that's been stabled too long,' Frances complained half in earnest and half in jest from the depths of her comfortable chair. 'What's the problem?'

'What makes you think that I have a problem?' Megan counter-questioned her cousin guardedly, her body tense and her hands clenching the varnished wooden rail so tightly that the muscles in her forearms ached.

'We've come a long way together,' Frances reminded her quietly. 'I know when something is bothering you, and you should know by now that you can trust me.'

'I *do* trust you, Frances, but I've got myself involved in a tricky situation, and——'

'It's Chad McAdam, isn't it?'

Megan should have known that Frances would guess at the truth, and, raising her hands in a gesture of despair, she turned to face her cousin's shadowy figure in the chair. 'Yes,' she sighed, 'it's Chad McAdam.'

Frances was silent for a moment before she said quietly, 'Do you want to talk about it?'

'Chad is in Johannesburg on business,' Megan began wearily, 'but before he left he told me he'd be sending his company's plane up to Izilwane in the morning with a load of veterinary equipment, and since I have to present my illustrations to the publishing company before lunch tomorrow he suggested that I take the plane on its return trip to Johannesburg.'

'And then, I presume, you'll drive back to Izilwane with Chad when you've both concluded your business,' Frances grasped the situation.

'Yes, that's correct.'

'It sounds like a sensible idea to me. Why drive all the way down to Johannesburg when you can fly down and get a lift back with Chad, so what's the problem?'

'The problem is, there's more to Chad's offer than a simple matter of transportation,' Megan confessed as she returned to her chair and sat down heavily. 'You see, I—I jumped in at the deep end like an idiot, and I'm not sure how much longer I'll be able to stay afloat.'

'In other words, Chad has been angling for an affair, but you've been avoiding the bait. You love him and, loving him as much as you do, you don't know how much longer you'll be able to resist the temptation.'

Frances had summed up the situation with her usual bluntness, striking more than one target, and Megan was glad she could not see her burning cheeks in the darkness.

'I've made my feelings pretty obvious, haven't I,' Megan responded drily, and not without a certain amount of embarrassment.

'Only to those of us who know you so well,' Frances assured her gravely. 'Have you ever considered the possibility that Chad might want something more than an affair?'

'He's always made it perfectly clear that marriage is out as far as he's concerned—so what else *is* there?' Megan demanded with a ring of unaccustomed bitterness in her soft voice.

'People have been known to change, Megan.'

'Not Chad!' Megan's laugh was mirthless and verging on tears. 'Oh, lord, Frances!' She buried her face briefly in her hands in a conscious effort to control herself. 'Tell me what I'm supposed to do?'

'What do *you* want to do?' Frances parried her query, and Megan took a moment to consider this before she answered her cousin.

'I think, deep down, I want to accept his offer of a flight down to Johannesburg. I want to meet with him and talk with him, and I want to take my chances on where it might lead me, but my mind warns against it.' She jumped up again and stepped towards the railing, gripping it tightly with her hands. 'I have a feeling that this meeting with Chad is going to be a crisis point in my life, and I'm not sure I'm ready for it. I don't want to lose what we've had together, and I'm terrified I might do something which will result in exactly that.'

Megan was startled by her own disclosure, and she lapsed into an embarrassed silence, expecting her cousin to laugh at her, but Frances was not laughing while she sat there staring out across the moonlit garden.

'Is Chad expecting you to call him this evening?'

Megan turned from her contemplation of the night sky to focus her attention on her cousin's shadowy figure in the darkness. 'Yes, he is,' she confessed quietly.

'Don't delay it, Megan. Call him now,' Frances suggested unexpectedly. 'Sometimes, when you love someone, you have to take chances. Go to him, find out what he wants, and then decide what you have to do.'

Megan hesitated only for a moment, and then she was going into the house and picking up the receiver of the telephone in the hall. She knew Chad's number at the office, she had stared at it often enough during this past week to know it off by heart, and she punched it out with a hand that shook slightly. She might not be quite ready for it, but Frances had made her realise that there was only one way to deal with this problem. She had to meet this crisis head-on.

The telephone barely rang before Chad answered it, making Megan suspect that he had been waiting at his desk for her call, and she somehow felt guilty for making him wait so long.

'Chad, it's Megan,' she said, her voice cool and calm despite the nervous thudding of her heart.

'What have you decided?' he demanded without preamble.

'I'd like to accept your offer to take that flight down to Johannesburg in the morning.' Was that a sigh of relief she heard coming over the line, or had it been her imagination?

'Very well,' he said briskly, interrupting her speculative thoughts. 'The plane should arrive at Izilwane at about nine tomorrow morning, and it will leave again as soon as the equipment is off-loaded. The pilot has been informed that he might be carrying a passenger on the return flight, and all you have to do is to make sure that you're at the airstrip by nine-thirty for his departure.'

'I'll be there,' Megan promised.

'Have you made a hotel reservation for yourself?'

'Yes, I have.'

'I presume you'll be staying at the same hotel as last time?'

'Yes.'

'Fine!' There was an odd silence at the other end as if Chad wanted to add something, and changed his mind. 'I'll be at the Rand airport to meet you, Megan, and I hope you have a pleasant flight,' he ended their brief conversation.

'Well?' Frances demanded curiously when Megan returned to her chair on the veranda.

'It's settled,' Megan told her cousin moments later with a shiver of nervous excitement coursing through her veins. 'I have to be at the airstrip at nine-thirty tomorrow morning.'

'What's this about having to be at the airstrip tomorrow morning?' demanded Byron as he stepped out on to the veranda.

Megan explained briefly and ended with a slightly breathless, 'I must go home and pack.'

'I'll drive you out to the airstrip in the morning,' he offered as they walked Megan to her car.

'That's kind of you, Byron.'

'Good luck,' whispered Frances before Megan could get into her white Mazda.

'Thanks,' Megan whispered back as she slid behind the wheel and turned the key in the ignition. 'I think I'm going to need it!'

CHAPTER TEN

THE PILOT was curious about the cargo he was ferrying back to Johannesburg, Megan could see it in the way he glanced at her from time to time, but there was nothing offensive in his manner, and his conversation whiled away the time during a flight which took less than an hour as opposed to the five-hour journey by car from Louisville.

Chad was at the airport to meet her, and he was an awesome stranger in his dark grey business suit and blue and grey striped tie when he stepped forward to relieve the pilot of the task of helping her to descend from the eight-seater plane. Megan shivered inside her suede coat, and she could not decide whether to blame it on the icy breeze sweeping across the tarmac or the commanding presence of the man beside her who exchanged a few words with the pilot before he ushered her towards the long silver-grey limousine parked a short distance away.

A black man in a grey suit and peaked cap opened the rear door when they approached, and Megan's mouth felt curiously dry as she preceded Chad into the warm, air-conditioned interior of the car. Her suitcase and portfolio containing her illustrations were stowed in the boot, and a few minutes later they were leaving the airport grounds and driving west towards the centre of the city.

'I wasn't expecting to be met in such style,' Megan remarked teasingly, stretching her legs out for comfort in the spacious interior of the limousine while she admired the plush upholstery and the many other luxurious additions which would be beyond the reach of a low-level executive.

'I'm trying to impress you,' Chad responded in the teasing vein she had adopted, his hand going out to the control panel beside him. He pressed one of the buttons, and Megan had to quell a nervous giggle when a panel slid silently into position to give them absolute privacy from the chauffeur in the driver's seat.

'I'm impressed,' she assured him gravely, but her blue eyes sparkled with laughter, making a mocking contradiction of her statement.

Chad's smiling glance captured hers and held it for a moment, but his expression sobered as he reached for her hand across the armrest between them.

'I'm glad you agreed to take this flight,' he said, his pale eyes probing hers as he raised her hand to brush his lips against the inside of her wrist in a brief, electrifying caress.

'I am too,' she confessed, her fingers curling about his in an involuntary response, and she noticed for the first time the strained, tired look about his eyes and mouth. 'You look as if you've had a tough week, and judging from the way you're dressed, it isn't over yet.'

'I'm going to be dropped off at Aztec.' His deep voice was clipped, and his fingers tightened about hers to convey an inner tension. 'I still have some unfinished business to attend to, but the car is at your disposal for the rest of the day, and Reggie, the chauffeur, has instructions to take you wherever you want to go.'

'You're being very kind and very generous.'

'I'm never kind, and I'm generous only when I want something in return.'

Megan stiffened beneath those strong fingers tracing the delicate network of veins at her wrist, but she could not stop that electrifying sensation that shot up her arm to make her nerve ends quiver in delight. 'I can't give you anything you don't have, or haven't had already.'

'I have a feeling you can give me something no one has given me before, but I can't quite decide what it is.'

She searched her mind for a clever response, but encountered a bewildering blank, and Chad's soft, throaty laughter did nothing to lift her from the well of confusion she had dropped into. What could she possibly give him that no one had given him before?

They were approaching the city centre when he released her hand to press the appropriate button on the control panel, and the division between the front and rear of the vehicle slid down silently into its cushioned recess.

Megan clasped her hands nervously in her lap and looked out the tinted window. The sound of the city traffic was muted inside the car, but to be surrounded by so much activity was enough to make her wish herself back at Izilwane, and she concentrated instead on the varying architectural design of the buildings. Some had been preserved as historical monuments and dated back to 1915, but others, sandwiched in between, were modern and perhaps more practical in their design. The old and the new seemed to blend without detracting from their own individual style, and the artist in Megan delighted in the perfect symmetry.

Reggie brought the vehicle to a stop at a busy intersection and, when the traffic lights changed, he turned left towards a tall, grey building with AZTEC emblazoned above the entrance. It was an impressive concrete and steel structure, but there was something cold and impersonal about it which did not appeal to Megan.

Chad leaned forward in his seat before the chauffeur could turn off into the parking bay for officials near the entrance. 'You can drop me off here, Reggie.'

'Yes, sir.'

The car pulled up at the kerb, and Chad took Megan's hand and raised it briefly to his lips before he opened the door and got out. 'I'll see you at the hotel this evening.'

She nodded, wanting to question the curious expression that had flitted across his face, but he was closing the door and striding towards the entrance before she could say anything. The navy-clad security guard raised his hand to his peaked cap in a salutary greeting, and moments later the swinging glass door closed behind Chad, obscuring him from view.

'Where do you wish me to take you, madam?'

Megan looked up with a guilty start, meeting the chauffeur's dark, questioning eyes in the rear-view mirror, and she hastily gave him the address.

John Driscoll's publishing house was several blocks away, and it was not as impressive as the Aztec Corporation's building, but the mixture of stone and whitewashed plaster had a warm, welcoming look about it.

Reggie parked the silver-grey limousine below the shallow steps leading up to the entrance and, leaving the engine running, he got out to open the door for Megan. 'What time shall I call for you, madam?' he asked as he handed her the portfolio she had requested from the boot.

'I doubt that I'll have concluded my business here before four o'clock this afternoon. Would that time suit you?' she asked with a measure of uncertainty.

Reggie smiled and raised his fingers respectfully to the polished peak of his cap. 'I'll be here at four, madam.'

There was no delay at reception. Megan was expected, and she took the lift up to the administrative offices on the eighth floor. The publisher's elderly secretary rose behind her desk with a smile of recognition and ushered her directly into the office behind the panelled door.

John Driscoll was a lean, wiry man in his early fifties, and he approached Megan from behind his desk with his usual brisk tread, his hands outstretched.

'Come in, Megan! Come in!' he welcomed her heartily, the grip of his fingers firm and a smiling warmth in the dark eyes surveying her from behind rimless spectacles. 'Could we offer you a cup of tea, perhaps?'

Megan's soft mouth curved in an answering smile. 'That would be nice, thank you.'

'Please arrange for a tray of tea, Mrs Simms, and make it three cups,' he asked his secretary. 'I'm expecting Wendy van Wijk to arrive shortly.'

'Certainly, Mr Driscoll.'

The panelled door closed behind Mrs Simms' grey-clad figure, and the publisher hastily cleared a space on his cluttered mahogany desk.

'Let's have a quick preview of your work while we wait for the author, shall we?' he suggested with almost childlike curiosity.

Megan removed the canvas board paintings, one by one, from her portfolio to put them on the desk for his inspection, but her mind was elsewhere. She was thinking about Chad, and wondering again what had been behind that fleeting but curious expression she had seen on his face when he had left her in the car to enter the Aztec building. What had it meant?

'This is absolutely marvellous work, Megan!' John Driscoll's enthusiastic statement made her surface from her thoughts to see him working his way once more through the pile of thirty illustrations, taking care not to disturb their order. 'Absolutely marvellous!' he said again.

'I think they're pretty good myself,' Megan admitted with a smile, 'but we won't know for sure until Mrs van Wijk has given them her seal of approval.'

'You're quite right, of course.' John Driscoll grimaced theatrically. 'Authors can be terribly fussy when it comes to the illustrative side of their work.'

'I don't blame them,' she retorted generously in defence of the author. 'The entire concept of Mrs van Wijk's story could be affected if the illustrations aren't compatible to the theme.'

'Just so, just so,' he agreed, glancing impatiently at his wrist watch, and just then the panelled door opened to admit the author and Mrs Simms, who was carrying the tray of tea he had ordered.

The day dragged for Megan, but it had its compensations. Wendy van Wijk could not fault Megan's illustrations, they were exactly what she had wanted, and that was when the tiresome but necessary paperwork commenced. There were contracts which had to be discussed and signed, and an agreement with the author that Megan would illustrate her next two books.

After a lavish two-hour lunch at a restaurant not far away, they returned to the publishing house to conclude their business, which had not been resolved without a measure of friction. Wendy van Wijk had had rigid ideas about what she wanted, but so had John Driscoll, and Megan had been caught uncomfortably between the two, constantly attempting to take the edge off their heated arguments until she had felt as if she was shrivelling with exhaustion inside her cerise-pink outfit.

Chad's silver-grey limousine was there at four o'clock to collect her and, leaving her empty portfolio in Reggie's hands, she slid thankfully into the warm interior of the car. She wondered yet again about Chad. Was he still at the Aztec Corporation offices, or had he gone home? She did not dare ask Reggie, and, closing her tired eyes, she leaned back comfortably in the cushioned seat while the car purred its way through the busy Johannesburg streets. What she needed was a cup of strongly brewed tea followed by a relaxing soak in a hot bath, and she could not wait to get to the hotel.

'You're on the tenth floor, Miss O'Brien,' the girl at the reception desk informed her when she arrived at the hotel fifteen minutes later. 'Take this lady's luggage up to the Duchess Suite, Alfred,' she added, turning to the porter and handing him the keys.

'There must be some mistake,' Megan protested confusedly. 'I didn't ask for the Duchess Suite.'

The girl checked the computer scanner and shook her head gravely. 'There's no mistake, Miss O'Brien, you're booked into the Duchess Suite. It's one of our best, and I'm sure you'll find it to your satisfaction, but please don't hesitate to give us a call if there's anything else you might need.' Her polite, enquiring glance shifted to the stocky, grey-haired man approaching the desk. 'May I help you, sir?'

Megan hesitated with indecision before she followed the porter across the foyer and into the lift. She had a feeling that Chad was responsible for her booking being changed to one of the luxury suites on the tenth floor, and she was fuming with anger. He had had no right to do something like this without discussing it with her, and she was going to tell him exactly what she thought of him when she saw him that evening!

The Duchess Suite was everything its name suggested, and it was furnished in the style of the eighteenth century, the colours ranging from a deep pearly pink to rich cream and gold. Megan tipped the porter and wandered through the lounge into the bedroom where the queen-sized bed with its elaborately draped canopy matched the style of the furniture in the lounge.

This was a luxury she had never allowed herself on her trips to Johannesburg, it was a waste when all she virtually needed was a place to sleep, but, mellowed by the splendour of her surroundings, she returned to the lounge and helped herself to a tot of port from the bar refrigerator in preference to the cup of tea she had wanted earlier.

She glanced at her watch. She still had plenty of time before dinner to bath and wash her hair and, kicking off her shoes, she lowered herself into a high-backed chair. She sipped her port and tried to relax, but the muscles in her body were still achingly taut half an hour later when she ventured into the bathroom to run her bath water. Her thoughts had revolved relentlessly around Chad, and none of her thoughts had encouraged relaxation.

She was sitting in front of the mirrored dressing-table in her half-slip and bra, drying her hair, when the telephone rang shortly after six that evening. That will be Chad, she thought, switching off her dryer and getting up to answer the phone. She had been waiting for his call, planning what she would say, but in the interim her anger had simmered down to nothing more than a vague annoyance.

'I hope you haven't had a tiring day, Megan?' he asked, his deep, velvety voice sending shivers of pleasure cascading through her.

'It was tiring, but it was successful, thank you.'

'Have you settled in comfortably? Is your accommodation to your satisfaction?'

'I'm more than comfortable, thank you,' she answered him stiffly, and then she could no longer contain her curiosity. 'Did you change my reservation to the Duchess Suite?'

'Yes,' he confirmed her suspicions. 'I thought it would be nice if you had the suite next to mine.'

Megan's legs caved in beneath her, and she sat down heavily on the bed. 'You're *here*? In *this* hotel?'

'I'm in the Somerset Suite.'

The Somerset and Duchess suites adjoined each other, Megan had noticed that on her arrival, and suddenly she knew the reason for that odd look she had seen on Chad's face that morning.

'Why are you staying here and not at your home?' she asked warily.

'I'll explain later,' he brushed aside her query abruptly. 'Will you join me in my suite for a drink before dinner?'

Megan felt a quick stab of uneasiness, but she shrugged it off just as quickly to ask, 'What time?'

'I'd like to shower and change into something else, so let's make it seven o'clock.'

'I'll see you at seven, then.'

Megan dressed with care that evening. Her soft woollen evening dress was a pastel shade of apricot that accentuated what was left of her summer tan. The sleeves were wide and gathered into a broad band at the wrist, and the neckline plunged just far enough to leave her respectability intact. The diamond studs in her ears and the matching pendant about her throat had been a gift from her parents three years ago on her twenty-first birthday, and they added the final touch to her appearance.

She studied herself absently in the full-length mirror, her glance trailing from the sheen of the fair hair curling softly about her face down to the delicate straps of the gold sandals on her feet. She looked calm and confident, but inwardly she was a bundle of nerves, and she pulled a face at herself before she turned away from the mirror. It was seven o'clock and, collecting her wrap and evening purse where she had put them in readiness on the bed, she left her suite.

Chad opened the door to the Somerset Suite almost immediately in response to her knock. There was still a trace of dampness in the dark hair which had been brushed back so severely from his broad forehead, and the familiar smell of his shaving cream and cologne wafted out towards her to attack her senses. She had wanted to appear cool and unruffled, but her heart was suddenly thudding uncomfortably hard against her ribs.

Her gaze dropped to the pearly buttons on his white silk shirt, but his compelling glance drew hers like a magnet, and she looked up to find him observing her with an amused expression in his eyes. He *knew* she was nervous! He had always had that uncanny ability to sense her thoughts and her feelings, and at that moment she could almost hate him for it.

'Come in, Megan.'

His hand emerged from the pocket of his black, expensively tailored trousers and, reaching out, he gripped her wrist and drew her inside. Caught off her guard, Megan was unresisting, and a thousand nerves leapt to attention as her body touched his. She tried to step back, but his hand shifted to the hollow of her back, deliberately prolonging this moment of intimacy, and her flush of embarrassment simply added to the amusement lurking in his eyes.

'Make yourself comfortable,' he suggested, but she was feeling extremely *un*comfortable with his hand in the small of her back as he guided her towards a high-backed chair which belonged to a set similar to the one in her suite.

She sat down, relieved to escape his disturbing touch, and her wary glance followed him when he walked towards the table beside the ornamental fireplace where a bottle of champagne nestled in a bucket of ice. The wrapper had been removed, and Chad lifted the bottle from its bed of ice to ease the cork from the slender neck. It shot out into his hand, the sound of its release jarring her raw nerves, and she jumped visibly.

'What are we celebrating?' she asked, trying desperately to regain her composure while she watched him pouring the fizzy liquid into two tall champagne glasses.

'Success,' he announced, his smile mocking as he turned to hand her a glass. 'You did say you had a successful day, didn't you?'

'Yes, very successful,' she confirmed, tasting her champagne and wishing he would sit down instead of towering over her. 'And you?' she asked. 'Did you have a successful day?'

'I concluded a deal which will swell the coffers of the Aztec Corporation, and the sale of my father's house was finalised. I sold it lock, stock and barrel, and the new owner moved in this afternoon.'

So this was why he was staying in the hotel, Megan thought with a stab of sympathy. 'It must have been a sad moment for you to have to part with your home.'

His wide shoulders moved beneath the silk shirt as if he wanted to shrug off her statement, and he sat down at last, giving her more room to breathe. 'It was senseless holding on to a place like that when it was so seldom in use, and it doesn't hold many happy memories for me.'

His twisted smile tugged savagely at her compassionate, loving heart, and she looked away, veiling her eyes with her gold-tipped lashes for fear he might mock her feelings.

'What do you have on your agenda for tomorrow?' he asked, breaking the contemplative silence between them.

'Absolutely nothing, and it's a glorious feeling.'

'We'll have the day to ourselves, then,' he said, leaving his chair and lifting the bottle of champagne from its icy nest to top up their glasses.

A nervous laugh escaped Megan when he returned to his chair. 'I don't usually drink this much champagne,' she explained when he glanced at her.

'Tonight is special.' He saw the wariness in her eyes before she could mask it, and an unfathomable expression flitted across his lean, handsome face. 'Let's take each moment as it comes, Megan. Shall we?'

Sometimes, when you love someone, you have to take chances. Frances' remark filtered unbidden through Megan's mind, and she forced herself to lower her guard a fraction.

'We'll take each moment as it comes,' she agreed quietly.

Chad's eyes creased into a smile devoid of mockery, and the melting warmth that surged through her seemed to turn her bones to liquid when they raised their glasses to each other in a silent toast.

It was much later that evening, when they were dining in the hotel's *à la carte* restaurant, that the tension eased from Megan's body to leave her relaxed as she faced Chad across the candlelit table in a wood-pillared alcove. Her reserve had crumbled somewhere between the salmon *pâté* and the crême caramel dessert, and she was responding to his gentle gibes and probing queries with her own particular brand of humour when their coffee was served.

A three-piece band had provided the music which had coaxed the couples on to the dance floor during courses, but Megan was content to listen and allow her thoughts freedom to wander while they drank their coffee.

There was something about Chad that set him apart from every other man in the room, and it had nothing to do with the expensive cut of his black velvet dinner jacket which accentuated the powerful width of his shoulders. It was perhaps that look of confidence and subdued aggression that drew the attention, but Megan was recalling instead her thoughts on that first occasion she had seen him more than a year ago. He was the best-looking man she had ever met, and she knew she was not the only one who thought so. Women had stared at him all evening, some openly, others covertly, and Chad had been aware of it. That cynical, faintly contemptuous look had flashed in his eyes a few times, and it had not been directed at Megan.

'Come, Megan, let's dance,' he suggested unexpectedly when the music changed from a disco beat to a slow, romantic number, and Megan allowed herself to be drawn to her feet.

He did not release her hand as they made their way among the tables, and then his hand was resting in the hollow of her back to guide her expertly across the floor in time to the slow, throbbing rhythm of the music. Megan had never danced with Chad before, but it was not the possibility of missing a step that made her stiffen against the guiding pressure of his hand. It was the closeness of their bodies, and the manly scent of his cologne, that was giving her cause for alarm. Her pulse rate had quickened to leave her flushed and faintly breathless, and she did not need to look at Chad to know that he was aware of the way his nearness was affecting her.

A member of the band crooned the words of a love song into the microphone, and Megan sighed inwardly. She would never forget her feelings for Chad, and neither could she ignore them at that moment as her body yielded against his, loving the feel of his taut thighs against her own when his arm tightened about her waist to draw her closer.

'I've wanted to hold you close like this from the moment you stepped off the plane this morning,' he murmured into her ear.

'What stopped you?' she mocked him.

'Uncertainty.' He raised his head to look at her and she sensed that the mockery in his eyes was directed at himself. 'It might help if I knew where I stood with you, but I don't understand myself lately, and it's a damned uncomfortable feeling.'

'I told you at the very beginning that it would be best for you to leave me alone and find someone else,' she reminded him. 'I could point out at least five women in this restaurant who'd give almost anything if you would so much as glance in their direction.'

'There's only one woman in this restaurant I'm interested in, and that's you, Megan,' he murmured throatily, the mockery leaving his eyes as he lowered his head to brush his lips against her temple. 'I don't happen to want anyone else.'

'You've got a problem,' she agreed with a certain gravity.

'I'm well aware of that, but what I need to know is how I'm going to solve it.'

Megan could not help him. She was having difficulty solving her own emotional problems, but, unlike Chad, she was acquainted with her feelings.

'The answer to your problem lies within yourself,' she said when the dance ended. 'All you have to do is find it.'

'How long does it take to find a needle in a haystack?' he laughed shortly, releasing her only to place a firm hand beneath her elbow as they returned to their table.

Chad did not expect an answer from her, and neither did she give him one. He held the key to what was locked away in his heart and his mind, and only he could use it.

They left the restaurant moments later, and Megan was in a mellow, relaxed mood when Chad followed her into her suite and closed the door. She had perhaps had too much wine with her dinner, she was not going to deny that, but she knew no sense of fear as she deposited her wrap and evening purse on a chair and turned to find him observing her with a curious expression in his steely eyes.

'It's been a lovely evening.' She was smiling as she reached up spontaneously to kiss him briefly on the lips in much the same way she might have kissed her father. 'Thank you, Chad.'

A look of surprise flashed across his handsomely chiselled features, but it was replaced swiftly by something dark and dangerously exciting.

'Megan!' Her name was an animal-like growl deep in his throat as he pulled her roughly into his hard arms. 'Oh, Megan!'

His mouth possessed hers, and his hands moved convulsively against her back, crushing her body to his as he kissed her with an oddly desperate passion. The velvet of his jacket was soft against her palms when her arms slid up about his neck, and she kissed him back with a fierce, unbridled passion of her own that left her feeling peculiarly drained when his arms finally slackened about her.

'I'm sorry if I was rough with you, but I needed this,' he murmured thickly, his fiery mouth trailing an exciting path across her jaw and down along the sensitive cord of her throat.

'So did I,' she heard herself confessing in a breathless, unrecognisably husky voice.

She slid her hands inside his jacket where she could feel the heat of his body through the silk of his shirt, and touching him like that awakened her to an urgent need to be closer still to this man she loved so much. Her hands moved almost of their own volition to explore the muscled wall of his chest, her fingers encountering his hardened male nipples through the silk, and his body grew taut against her, alerting her to the danger of what she was doing.

It thrilled her to know she had the power to arouse Chad, but it also scared her sufficiently to bring her to her senses. His mouth stilled against her throat as if he had sensed her mental rather than her physical withdrawal, and he lifted his dark head to kiss her on the tip of her small, straight nose before he released her to flick an admonishing finger against her flushed cheek.

'I'll see you in the morning, Megan,' he smiled twistedly, and then he left.

Megan went into the bedroom and started to undress, but Chad's presence seemed to linger with her, the remembered warmth and smell of him filling her with a longing which remained with her until she finally went to sleep from sheer exhaustion.

CHAPTER ELEVEN

THE FOLLOWING day dawned clear and sunny, but there was a slight nip in the air as a reminder that autumn would soon make way for winter. Chad had suggested at the breakfast table that they spend the day in the country, and Megan could not fault the idea when the hotel staff offered to pack them a picnic lunch. They visited several places of interest, but their final destination was the Hartebeespoort dam, which lay forty kilometres west of Pretoria.

The road eventually passed through a tunnel before it became a single lane across the dam wall which closed a narrow *nek* in the Magaliesberg to impound the Crocodile River, and Megan glanced about her with interest. 'I've never been here before,' she confessed.

Chad glanced at her briefly and smiled. 'This was one of my favourite hunting grounds.'

Megan wondered what nature of hunting he was referring to, but she chose not to question him about it. She did not want anything to mar this day for her.

Chad hired a powerboat for the day, and she enjoyed the thrill of speeding across the fifteen square kilometres of the reservoir with the fine spray of the water on her face and the wind whipping through her hair. She was in no particular hurry for Chad to end this exhilarating chase after nothing in particular, and she was content to sit and watch the play of muscles in his sun-browned arms where he stood with his hands resting firmly on the controls.

The wind swept his dark hair away from his broad forehead, and flattened his blue shirt against his body to accentuate his muscled chest and taut, flat stomach above the leather belt hugging his grey denims to his hips. He was exuding an air of aggressive masculinity that stirred her senses, and that was only one of the many reasons why she loved him. Beneath that cold, cynical and often embittered exterior she had glimpsed a warm, gentle and caring man; a man with a need to give and receive love like anyone else, but that side of him had been forcibly suppressed since his youth.

Trusting a woman will never come easy to a man as cynical as Chad McAdam. That was what Glenys Gibson had said, and Megan knew the reason why. She had not sat with him all those hours through his bout of malaria without learning something of his pain and his fears, but she was not sure that it was within her power to teach him to trust again.

She shelved her thoughts hastily as Chad pointed to a secluded spot up ahead of them, and the silence was almost deafening when he finally moored the boat and cut the engine.

'This is one of the few places in and around the city where one can get really close to nature,' he said some minutes later when he had deposited their picnic basket in a cool spot and was lowering himself on to the rug Megan had spread out beneath a shady tree along the embankment. 'My father was a member of the Yacht Club, and I used to come here often as a child. I would pretend that I was a hunter stalking animals in the bush with my rifle in search of a trophy to hang on my wall at home, but when I grew older I used to sit here to dream about the future when I'd be qualified to heal the animals I'd wanted to slay in my childhood.'

This explained his curious statement about the dam being one of his favourite hunting grounds, and Megan almost laughed out loud at what she had imagined he had meant.

'Do you see your post at Izilwane as the fulfilment of your dreams?' she asked, studying his strong profile as she sat down beside him, and allowing her glance to linger on the straight, high-bridged nose, the sensuous mouth and strong, jutting jaw.

'Yes, I do, and I'm looking forward to the time when my trips to the city will be limited to the Aztec Corporation's quarterly board meetings.' He turned his head, capturing her glance, and an unexpected gleam of mockery entered his eyes. 'I've told you before, it's time I settled down with a woman...or two...or three.'

'Three sounds like a nice number with which to start off your harem,' she agreed lightly, averting her gaze and staring out across the wide expanse of water rippling in the sunlight.

'I shall have to collect them one at a time.' He cupped her chin in his hand and turned her face back to his, forcing her to look at him. 'At the moment I'm still concentrating on you.'

His hand slid round to the nape of her neck, his fingers curling into the short, honey-gold hair, and he leaned towards her, capturing her mouth with his and silencing the caustic reply which had risen to her lips. He kissed her playfully, his mouth teasing and tantalising hers to arouse a deep-seated hunger for more, and then, suddenly, his kisses were no longer playful. They were urgent and demanding, and Megan found herself meeting that demand with a surprising urgency of her own as he bore her down on to the rug and held her there with the weight of his body.

Her arms went up of their own volition to become locked about his strong neck, and she clung to him, her fingers curling into the cotton of his shirt in an attempt to steady herself in this dizzying world of escalating emotions. Warnings flashed through her mind, but they faded swiftly when Chad trailed a delicious path of fiery kisses along her jaw to her throat, and then he was once again ravaging her eager, quivering mouth to drive her closer towards that ragged edge where sanity no longer prevailed.

'Your lips taste like honey, and you always smell like a fresh mountain breeze,' he murmured thickly when he eased his mouth from hers to bury his face against her throat. 'I like it.'

Megan had gone beyond the point of searching for a flippant response to ease the emotional tension between them. She could feel the heat of his hands on her body through her khaki slacks and amber-coloured blouse, and his touch excited her, but she came to her senses when she felt him undoing the buttons of her blouse.

'No, don't...please!' she protested weakly, gripping his strong, sinewy wrists in an attempt to stay his action, but the last button gave way beneath his fingers, and the front of her blouse was parted to expose the lacy bra which was her only protection. 'Don't, Chad!' she pleaded huskily, looking up into pale eyes with black pinpoints of fire in their depths. 'Someone might see us! Please don't do this to me!'

'There's no one anywhere near us, this place is deserted during the week, and I want to look at you and touch you.'

His throaty reply heightened her fear, but he held her a prisoner beneath his aroused body, making her struggles ineffectual while he unhooked the front catch of her bra and peeled aside the lacy material to expose her small, pointed breasts. Megan's cheeks flamed, and she raised her hands to use them as a shield, but Chad wrenched them away to imprison them above her head. She could not lie there placidly for his inspection, and she writhed beneath his aroused body in a desperate attempt to escape, but there was something in the way he looked at her that suddenly stilled her actions.

'You're so beautiful, Megan!'

The raw emotion in his voice matched the look on his face when he bowed his dark head in something close to reverence over her breasts, circling one rosy peak with the tip of his moist tongue in an erotic caress before he took the hardened nipple into his hot mouth and sucked gently.

He did the same to her other breast, and Megan was not aware that she was holding her breath, but it finally escaped past her lips in a shuddering moan of pleasure which she had been incapable of suppressing. Her body was being awakened to sensations which were incredibly sweet and dangerously intense, and she did not shy away from it. Something inside her was beginning to want more, and she pushed her fingers through Chad's hair in a convulsive action, almost guiding his mouth when he repeated the action.

A wave of piercingly sweet desire swept through her, and it aroused an unfamiliar stab of aching, wanting warmth in her loins. It was a sobering experience, and she was forced to take a quick, sane look at herself. If Chad made love to her now she was afraid she might not have the will to stop him!

Her fears had been unnecessary. Chad drew the fronts of her blouse together to cover her nakedness, and sat up abruptly with his elbows resting on his knees, to leave her staring at his broad back.

She raised herself warily into a sitting position, temporarily at a loss to understand his behaviour, while she fastened the catch of her bra and buttoned up her blouse with hands that were shaking uncontrollably. Chad had had her exactly where he had always wanted her. He could have taken her if he had wanted to, but he had changed his mind. Why? She stared at his back which was turned so resolutely towards her, wanting to question him, but she was too bewildered and unsure of herself to speak.

'I think I must be going crazy.' He combed his fingers angrily through his dark hair and turned, one thigh resting heavily against hers as he subjected her to his narrowed, speculative gaze. 'Nothing has stopped me before from having a woman when and where I've wanted her, but with you it's different,' he said, his voice low and urgent as he answered her unspoken query. 'I've always been a taker, Megan. I take what's given and give nothing in return, but with you, the wanting and the giving has to be a mutual thing between us. Do you understand?'

'I understand perfectly.' She held his glance and felt herself driven by the need to explain. 'Chad, it—it isn't a lack of—of wanting.'

'I know.' There was a suggestion of the old mockery in his narrowed gaze. 'It's the *giving* that the old-fashioned side of you still objects to.'

'But I think ... at the right time and place ... anything is possible,' she finished off his remark on a daringly provocative note.

'That sounds encouraging.'

His glance had shifted to her lips, and she hastily changed the subject. 'Do you think we could eat? I'm starving!'

'So am I.'

The devilish gleam in his eyes told Megan that he was not talking about food, but she chose to ignore the implication of his remark, and Chad left the matter there to fetch the picnic basket.

The hotel kitchen had packed an enormous lunch of chicken portions, salads, crispy rolls, and a bottle of wine with two glasses. Megan did not think they would finish it all, but they talked while they ate, and two hours later the picnic basket contained only the remnants of their meal.

'This has been a memorable day,' she sighed as Chad poured the last of the wine into their glasses. 'I don't think I shall ever forget it.'

'Neither will I,' he echoed her statement as he dropped the empty bottle into the picnic basket. 'I've shared something with you today that I've never shared with any other woman before.'

Megan did not doubt his statement, but she was not going to allow herself to believe he thought she was special, and it was with that thought in mind that the flutter of hope in her breast was quelled.

The doves were calling in the trees while they sat in silence, drinking their wine, but the sun was beginning to set, and that wintry nip was filtering slowly into the air.

'It's time to go,' Chad announced when he saw Megan shiver, and a few minutes later they were bouncing across the water in the powerboat.

Chad did not open up the engine to full throttle when he returned the boat to its original moorings. It appeared he was as reluctant as Megan to end this day they had spent together, and a deep sadness welled up inside her when they finally drove away from the dam and headed back to Johannesburg.

At the dinner table that evening both Megan and Chad were aware that this was their last evening together in Johannesburg before they returned to Izilwane. Nothing had been resolved between them, but, in the aftermath of the pleasant day they had shared, they were both reluctant to touch on a subject which might arouse remembered friction.

'I'm going to have a three-bedroomed prefabricated cottage erected on that plot of ground up at Izilwane,' Chad announced when they were lingering at their table in the wood-pillared alcove over a second cup of coffee. 'I'm sure I could live there quite comfortably until I've had a proper house built, but I'd need someone to help me with the décor. Would you be interested?'

'There's a firm in Louisville who does this sort of thing professionally, but I'll help you if that's what you really want.'

He leaned forward in his chair and rested his elbows on the table. 'You're a fine artist and an adventurous businesswoman, but there's also something restful and homely about you, and that's the atmosphere I'm sure you'll help me to create.'

'I'll do my best,' she promised, sipping her coffee and studying him closely over the rim of her cup. 'What you really need is a wife.'

Chad's eyes flickered dangerously in the light of the candle between them. 'Are you applying for the post?'

'I wasn't aware that you were advertising.'

'You're sharp, and I like that.' His strongly chiselled features creased in a faintly amused smile. 'Tell me, Megan, why would I want to advertise for something I don't want?'

'Because you're not really the harsh, unfeeling man you want people to believe you are,' she explained quietly, holding his glance while she lowered her cup into the saucer. 'You've raised barriers to protect yourself from being hurt, but you're human enough to want someone there with you to ward off the loneliness.'

'And you think a wife could do that?' he demanded mockingly.

'I think,' she began cautiously, 'you need to re-assess life in general, and yours in particular.'

His shoulders moved beneath the black velvet dinner jacket as if she had touched a nerve. 'I've been doing a lot of re-assessing lately, but I haven't come up with the answers yet.'

The atmosphere changed abruptly, and there was an emotional tension in the air between them which refused to be ignored. Megan's eyes met Chad's, and suddenly her stable, rational world crumbled away beneath her feet until nothing and no one existed in the restaurant except Chad and her physical awareness of him as a man.

She could not recall how or when they left the crowded restaurant to take the lift up to the tenth floor, but she was aware of Chad's hands sliding over her body, stroking her into an awareness of her own need when they stood in the dimly lit corridor outside her suite.

'Let me stay with you tonight, Megan?'

His voice fell softly on her ears, and she wanted to say yes, but a part of her still held back. This was the crisis point she had feared. Her love for Chad had become a destructive weapon, and she was being torn apart inside.

'If you change your mind,' he said, sensing her indecision, 'You'll know where to find me.'

Megan did not want him to go. She wanted to call him back when he turned on his heel and walked away from her, but the words remained locked in her throat, and she fumbled the key into the lock to enter her suite.

Her mind was not on what she was doing when she went through the usual ritual of undressing, creaming off her make-up and brushing her teeth. She was thinking about Chad, and her physical need of him was so intense that her hand went out several times to the telephone on the cupboard beside her bed, but every time she snatched it back before her fingers could touch the receiver.

She had to think! She had to be sure! Was her need strong enough to silence the voice of her conscience?

This was the final chapter, Megan's heart warned her. This was a moment which she would have to grasp with both hands if she did not want to lose it forever.

If you change your mind you'll know where to find me.

She thrust her arms into the sleeves of her blue silk gown, fastening the belt about her waist while she pushed her feet into her soft mules, and then she was marching out of her suite and along the deserted corridor to knock on Chad's door before her courage deserted her.

The door was opened seconds later, and she passed the tip of her tongue nervously over her lips as she found herself face to face with Chad. He was wearing a green towelling robe that left his legs bare from the knees down, but it was not what he was wearing that interested her at that moment. His expression was inscrutable, but there was an oddly vulnerable look about his eyes and mouth which did not escape her. It stabbed her to the soul, and gave her the courage to go on.

'I've changed my mind,' she said unnecessarily, her heart thudding against her ribs.

'I was hoping you would,' he said, taking the hands she held out to him and drawing her inside.

'It wasn't an easy decision.'

'I know.' He closed the door, and the emotional tension spiralled between them as his eyes probed hers in the dimly lit room. He seemed to find what he was searching for, and then his taut features relaxed visibly. 'Oh, Megan!' Her name was a tortured groan on his lips. 'I want you so much that it's been driving me out of my mind!'

His fingers bit into her shoulders, and then he was sweeping her into his arms, crushing her small softness against the hard length of him with a force which threatened to drive the breath from her body. He rained fiery kisses on her face and throat before he sought her eager, waiting lips, and if there had still been the slightest doubt in Megan's mind then it was dispelled by the urgency of his kiss.

She wanted him so much that her body was aching with a need to be closer to him, and she could feel the muscles rippling beneath his robe as she slid her hands up across his broad back to cling to his shoulders as she ventured for the first time into this mad, ecstatic world of passion. This was going to be a precious moment in her life, and it would have to sustain her through to eternity.

'Make love to me, Chad,' she whispered urgently when his mouth left hers to seek out that erratic little pulse at the base of her throat, and he raised his dark head to look down into eyes which were almost feverishly bright with emotion.

'Are you sure that's what you want?'

'Yes, I'm sure.'

He hesitated for one heart-stopping moment, then he lifted her in his arms as if she were a child and carried her into the bedroom. His eyes were chips of steel with a dark fire leaping in their depths, and Megan wanted to lose herself in them, but Chad was brushing his lips across her eyelids as he lowered her on to her feet beside the bed.

Her gown and her flimsy nightdress fell almost unnoticed to the floor at her feet while his mouth made a sensuous exploration of the delicate contours of her face before it detoured down along the slender arch of her neck to her creamy shoulder. His mouth sought hers again in long, drugging kisses, and she could not recall when he removed his robe, but it came as a pleasurable shock to feel his naked, heated body against her own when he lifted her on to the enormous bed with its blue drapes and lay down beside her.

He made love to her slowly, his hands gentling her body until every nerve and sinew was quiveringly alert to his touch. He explored her sensitised flesh with his mouth and his hands, filling her senses with the taste and smell of him and igniting a fire inside her that made her impatient to be possessed.

'Oh, Chad!' she breathed his name unsteadily, her excitement mounting and her fingernails digging into the muscles stretching taut across his shoulders when he pushed his knee between hers to trail his hand along her inner thigh in search of the most intimate part of her body. 'I want you so much!'

Chad stayed the action of his hand when her trembling body arched involuntarily to meet his touch. 'What made you change your mind?' he asked throatily, his mouth seeking hers.

'Don't you know yet that I love you?'

The truth had spilled from her lips before she could prevent it, and she knew instantly that it had been a mistake. He stiffened against her, his head jerking up as if she had struck him, and the look on his face was frightening when he left her side with a muttered oath to shrug himself into his robe.

'Chad...please...I'm sorry.' Megan dragged the duvet up against her naked body and sat up in bed with a stricken look on her face as he tugged the curtains aside to stare out of the window. 'It doesn't have to change anything, does it?'

'It changes *everything*!' He tugged the curtains back across the window, shutting out the flickering city lights, and Megan shivered despite the air-conditioned warmth of the room when he turned to her with savage anger on his face. 'It changes everything for *me*!'

'Because I dared to say I love you?' she asked, her mouth suddenly so dry that she could scarcely raise her voice above a whisper while she fought against the pain and humiliation of his rejection.

'Yes!' He shot the word at her like a bullet out of a gun, and she flinched, her face whitening.

'I see,' she murmured, a cold, despairing anger coming to her rescue as she reached down on to the floor for her discarded nightdress and pulled it on over her head with as much dignity as she could muster.

'No, you *don't* see!' Chad was beside her in an instant, his eyes blazing with an inner fury and something else which she could not define when his hands closed about her shoulders like a vice to lift her off the bed and on to her feet. 'For heaven's sake, Megan, I've got to make you understand! Right up to the moment when you said you loved me there was still a part of me that wanted you and then wanted to be free of you!'

'Do you think I didn't know that?' she stormed at him in an anguished voice, her eyes dark with pain and misery and filling rapidly with tears. 'Don't you realise that it's *because* I love you so much that I decided to snatch this moment of happiness with you even though I knew it would be brief?'

Her insides were shaking, affecting her breathing, and through the film of her humiliating tears she saw a peculiar whiteness sliding up beneath the skin along Chad's jaw and about his mouth.

'You don't deserve this kind of treatment, and I think I've known that for a long time.' His voice was vibrant with an emotion she could not determine at that moment as he slackened his punishing grip on her shoulders. 'I'm glad I didn't make love to you now, and when I do, it must be because I have that right...as your husband.'

The room tilted crazily. This had to be a mad, impossible dream, but the touch of his warm hands on her shoulders was very real.

'Do you know what you're saying?' she croaked in disbelief, her legs threatening to cave in beneath her while she searched his face for the answer.

'I love you, Megan.' There was a break in his voice, telling her exactly how difficult it had been for a man like Chad to make that confession, but his tortured expression revealed a great deal more in that instant before he pulled her roughly into his arms. 'Heaven knows, I've been fighting a relentless battle with myself these past few months, and I've been going quietly out of my mind because of it, but I can't go on fighting against the truth. I don't just want your body, Megan, I want *all* of you, and it still scares the hell out of me, but...I want to marry you.'

Megan's heart stilled in her breast, then raced on at an incredible pace. This was reality, it was not a dream, she realised at last, and her happiness was so intense that she was suddenly laughing and crying at the same time as she flung her arms about his neck and buried her face against his broad chest.

'You don't know how much I've longed to hear you say those words, but I believed you never would,' she explained, her voice muffled and her tears dampening the front of Chad's towelling robe. 'Oh, lord!' she laughed shakily, failing in her attempt to wipe away her tears until a handkerchief was thrust into her hands. 'I know it's silly of me to cry, but I'm so happy that I—I just can't seem to help it.'

Chad stroked her silky hair, soothing her until she managed to control herself, but there was a tolerant, faintly amused smile hovering about his sensuous mouth as he slid his fingers beneath her chin and tipped her face up to his.

'Does this mean you'll marry me?' he asked, pocketing his damp handkerchief.

'Yes! Oh, *yes*, Chad!' she whispered tremulously, her eyes alight with happiness, but her expression sobered the next instant. 'If you're sure that's what you really want.'

'I know now that nothing else will suffice, but…' The muscle along his jaw grew taut, and there was a flash of remembered bitterness in his eyes. 'It will have to be for ever,' he concluded on a warning note.

Megan understood, and her compassionate, loving heart reached out to him. He had made himself vulnerable by admitting that he loved her, but the fear of being hurt was still there, and her expression was grave when she took him by the shoulders and pushed him down on to the bed.

'Nothing is ever going to make me leave you, Chad,' she assured him with a fierce honesty as she knelt between his thighs. 'Nothing! Do you understand? You can throw me out of your life, but I'll come back in again even if I have to hammer down doors to do it.' Her luminous eyes held his, allowing him to see into her heart and beyond while she gripped his hands tightly with the urgency of the message she was conveying. 'Trust me, Chad. Trust me with your love as I trust you with mine.'

His taut features relaxed slowly, and she could almost feel the tension draining from him before he lifted her on to the bed where he held her a willing prisoner beneath the weight of his body.

'As I recall, I once told you that to trust a woman would be as foolish as to come between a hungry lion and its prey.' He smiled wryly at the memory, and she felt the faint stubble of beard scraping her skin when he rubbed his cheek against hers. 'I think, since that time you nursed me when I had malaria, I've known that I need never feel that way with you.'

'Oh, Chad!' Her sigh was ecstatic, and she wrapped her arms around him and she opened her mouth to him with a hunger which he did not hesitate to satisfy.

Fate had woven a spell around them that day, and the magic was still there, sharpening their hunger into desire as they clung to each other a little wildly, their bodies straining to get closer, but this time there was an underlying tenderness in the knowledge that they loved each other.

'Let's not wait, Megan.' Chad's low, throaty voice excited her almost as much as his erotic tongue flicking across her heated flesh as it trailed a devastating path from her throat down to where the V of her nightdress exposed the gentle curve of her breasts. 'Let's get married tomorrow before we return to Louisville.'

'I wish I could say yes, but I can't.' Her eyes were slumbrous with the extent of her emotions as she curled her fingers into his hair to stay the action of his tantalising mouth while she still had the strength to do so. 'I have to think about my family. I'd like their blessing on our decision, and they've been so good to me over the years that it's only fair to include them in our plans.'

'Yes, you're right,' Chad agreed, the smoky fire of desire in his eyes subsiding and a rueful smile curving his sensuous mouth. 'I'm selfish and impatient, and I have no doubt that this period of waiting will be an agony of a different kind, but you deserve to have a white wedding with all the usual trimmings. Just don't make me wait too long, because I know I shan't rest until you're mine.'

'I won't make you wait too long. I promise we'll be married as soon as it can be arranged.' She smiled up at him tremulously, loving the feel of his warm, hard body against her own as she slid her fingers through his soft, springy hair, and down along his lean jaw to his strong, sunbrowned throat. 'Thank you for understanding.'

'Megan! My Megan!' His face darkened with remorse as he eased himself away from her and captured one of her hands in his to bury his warm mouth against her soft palm. 'You've had me on a leash from the start, tugging gently to bring me to my senses, and I hope that some day you'll forgive me for hurting you so much.'

'I've always tried to understand the reason behind the things you've said and done, and that makes forgiveness unnecessary,' she said simply and honestly.

'You're a remarkable woman.'

'I love you, Chad,' she whispered, her thigh brushing against his when she shifted her position slightly, and she felt his chest heave beneath her hands.

'Lying here like this with you is the next best thing to making love to you, but it's not very good for my blood pressure,' he growled, and there was a noticeable tremor in his hands when he rose to his feet and lifted her up with him. 'It must be after midnight, but I know I won't be able to sleep tonight, so let's pack up and get the hell out of here,' he suggested with an understandable urgency as he picked up her gown and helped her into it. 'Let's go home to Louisville.'

'I'll get dressed and pack the last few things.'

Megan had fastened the belt of her gown about her waist and was about to return to her suite when Chad caught her up against him in a fierce embrace which almost drove the breath from her body.

'I love you, Megan,' he groaned, and the words seemed to come so much easier this time. 'I swear I'll spend the rest of my life showing you just how much I love you.'

His warm mouth shifted over hers in a hard, satisfying kiss, and Megan prayed silently that she would always be worthy of his love.

Coming in July
From America's favorite author

JANET DAILEY

Fiesta San Antonio

Out of print since 1978!

The heavy gold band on her finger proved it was actually true. Natalie was now Mrs. Colter Langton! She had married him because her finances and physical resources for looking after her six-year-old nephew, Ricky, were rapidly running out, and she was on the point of exhaustion. He had married her because he needed a housekeeper and somebody to look after his young daughter, Missy. In return for the solution to her problems, she had a bargain to keep.

It wouldn't be easy. Colter could be so hard and unfeeling. "I don't particularly like myself," he warned her. "It's just as well you know now the kind of man I am. That way you won't expect much from our marriage."

If Natalie had secretly hoped that something would grow between them—the dream faded with his words. Was he capable of love?

Don't miss any of Harlequin's three-book collection of Janet Dailey's novels each with a Texan flavor. Look for *BETTER OR WORSE* coming in September, and if you missed *NO QUARTER ASKED*...